ONE CHANCE

The school was having some kind of fiesta. Crêpe paper streamers were strung across the basketball court and children and adults milled around refreshment stands. Quickly I scanned the crowd for Jane and Michael, but couldn't find them.

Then a familiar movement on the far side of the court caught my eye: a little boy and girl hugged each other, then the girl impatiently wriggled free. My fingers dug into the back of the old sofa I was sitting on.

"My babies!" I cried out. "My beautiful children!"

How I ached to run down and touch their hands through the steel fence. As it was, all I could do was look down at them and weep helplessly.

I had to wait for just the right moment. There was no room for mistakes.

I would only have this one chance to get them back.

WHERE ARE MY CHILDREN?

CASSIE KIMBROUGH

ZEBRA BOOKS
KENSINGTON PUBLISHING CORP.

For Jane and Michael
and
In Memory of Bob

ZEBRA BOOKS

are published by

Kensington Publishing Corp.
475 Park Avenue South
New York, NY 10016

First printing: September, 1991

Printed in the United States of America

The Kidnapping

Chapter One

Friday, November 13, 1987

It was six o'clock in the evening of Friday the thirteenth. I wasn't superstitious, but still it was a relief that the day was almost over, and nothing bad had happened.

My soon-to-be ex-husband, Federico, would be here any minute to pick up Jane and Michael. They were in their room choosing the toys they wanted to take on their weekend visit. Michael, four years old and all boy, was deciding which He-Man figure to take. Jane, six, looked up at me and asked, "Mommy, where's my Barbie doll?" She would be tall like me. What a contrast to her brother, who would have his father's dark hair and sturdier build.

There was a rap at the door, then a chorus of "Daddy! Daddy!" Federico swept Michael into the air and hugged Jane. I knew this display was partly for my benefit—he hadn't been this affectionate with the children before our separation—but I was glad they still had a loving relationship. In spite of the bitterness of our pending divorce and custody battle, it was my fervent hope that Federico's and my problems would remain just that—his and mine—and not spill over onto the children. But that hope seemed more and more unlikely as time went on.

Federico had demanded a jury trial to decide who should get custody of Jane and Michael. It was set for December, only a month away. I was pretty sure I would be granted custody, in spite of Federico's attempts to paint me as a bad mother. Still, the trial would be ugly. It would leave scars. Anyway, I thought with a sigh, it would be over soon. Then we could all pick up the pieces and live normal lives again.

"Don't forget you promised to take them to the matinee on Sunday to see 'The Ugly Duckling,' " I reminded Federico.

"Sure. I can buy the tickets from you now," he said. I could hear the forced amiability through his thick Spanish accent. Federico was Bolivian, although with his light skin and green eyes, he looked more European than Latin American. He paid for the tickets and pocketed them. The smile on his face was more like a smirk, but I considered it an encouraging sign anyway. Maybe things were settling down and he was regaining a margin of sanity. Was it my imagination, or had he been more cooperative for the past few weeks? Could I dare hope he would give up his insistence on a jury trial?

As I looked at him I found it hard to believe that this was the same man I had married nine years before. Nine years. Amazing, that two so very different people had stayed together that long. We had met at the University of Texas at Austin, and after a tempestuous courtship that had lasted two and a half years, we were married. Two weeks later we'd gone to Bolivia to live. Federico promised that we'd live there only two years. But the two years had stretched into six and a half. Finally, in 1985, we had come back to Texas. That was two years ago. Now here we were, two continents and two children later, strangers again.

I hugged Jane and Michael goodbye and shut the door behind them. Turning, I saw the toys they'd forgotten in the hubbub over their father's arrival. I shouted out the door at them and they came running back, Jane's dark blonde hair flying.

Quick hugs and they were gone again, this time clutching the toys as they ran down the sidewalk. Having a favorite plaything nearby would be a comfort when they woke up in an unfamiliar place, I thought. After all, they had spent the night with Federico only a few times since he'd moved out.

At first, he would pick them up on Saturday morning and have them back in time for supper. Lately, for some reason, he'd started keeping them all weekend. But I'd taken this increased paternal solicitude as a positive sign also.

Anyway, this weekend it would be convenient for me that the kids were gone. I was going to be busy with three performances of the ballet "The Ugly Duckling." In it, I played the role of the mother swan to a half dozen adolescent cignets. The first performance was that night.

I set about getting ready to go to the theater, pulling on tights and leotard and twisting my hair into a chignon. Jane and Michael had come with me to most of the rehearsals. They were excited now about seeing the full-fledged ballet, complete with costumes and scenery. I was probably every bit as nervous as the young girls who would be dancing on stage for the first time that night, but my excitement was tinged with sadness. After the Sunday matinee, this would be my last performance. The mother swan's swan song—the final laying to rest of a childhood dream.

At one time or another nearly every girl yearns to be a ballerina, but I might have had a chance to make that dream come true. When I was fourteen I had been offered a scholarship at a well-known ballet school. Daddy had been alarmed at the idea of his daughter going off to the big bad city all by herself. He'd been even more alarmed at the prospect of me, a lawyer's daughter, becoming a professional dancer. It was a narrow life, he'd said, grueling, competitive, mean. So I didn't go.

But my love for dance had persisted through the years, and I'd kept it up now and again between college and babies. But now the strenuous routine of class and rehearsal was just not possible anymore. I was thirty-four years old, not fourteen. Even so, age was not as much of a factor as the accoutrements that age brought with it: a job, children, responsibilities that took up all my time and energy. And soon I would be a single mother with even less free time. So I danced that Friday night with an awareness that it would be one of the last times.

Late that night, just before falling asleep, I remembered fleetingly again that it was Friday the thirteenth. It had passed without incident.

The next day was unseasonably warm for November—even for the semi-tropical climate of McAllen, Texas, in the Rio Grande Valley—and I kept thinking that the sweaters I'd packed for Jane and Michael would be too hot. I made a mental note to call Federico and go by his apartment with lighter clothes for them. Instead I was needed at the theater to sew last-minute feathers onto swan costumes. There were so many details to take care of for the ballet that night that I completely forgot about calling the kids. Saturday night's performance was important—it would be videotaped and all the local critics would be there—and the atmosphere at the theater was electric with anticipation. Except for a few wobbles here and there, everything went fairly well. There was a party afterward, but I went straight home from the theater, mindful of keeping my image pristine for the upcoming custody trial.

At the matinee performance on Sunday afternoon, as I waited in the wings for our cue to step onto the stage, a little thrill of pleasure went through me as I thought of Jane and Michael in the audience. "The Ugly Duckling" had turned out in performance to be delightful—touching and funny at the same time. They'd love it. Once on stage, though, I could see nothing but blackness beyond the footlights. I kept straining to hear Michael's voice piping "There's Mommy!" across the darkness. That had happened a few months earlier. I was a little relieved not to hear it this time.

As soon as I got home, my friend Susan called. She had gone to the matinee with her two young children. "It was adorable! My kids loved it. But," she added, "we didn't see Jane and Michael. They weren't there."

"Are you sure?"

"I'm positive. We went up and down the aisles looking for them during each intermission."

I was irritated. It would be just like Federico to buy tickets and then not take the kids, just to annoy me. This time I wasn't going to take the bait. I resisted the impulse to call him and demand an explanation. Besides, I had a hands-off policy for the weekends that Jane and Michael spent with him. It was their time together, and I made it a point not to interfere. So I didn't call.

By six o'clock that evening I was restless for them to be home. It was always like this on their weekends away. On the first day, I enjoyed the luxury of having time to myself. But by the second day, the apartment seemed empty without them, and I'd start to miss them.

Six-thirty came. No knock on the door. Well, he was always a little late. It was just another weapon in his arsenal of divorce one-upmanship. I waited awhile, then phoned his apartment. No answer. At seven-thirty there was still no answer. They were probably visiting one of his friends, I told myself. Nevertheless, a tiny, nagging worry began to grow in my mind.

The summer before, Federico had taken the children all the way to Miami to see his mother and sister who had flown up from Bolivia, and he'd brought them back safe and sound. At the time Douglas Rothenthal, my lawyer, had said I wasn't under any legal obligation to let Federico take Jane and Michael with him. But I didn't want to cut them off from their Bolivian relatives. And Federico was planning to take them to Disney World — every child's dream come true. Besides, I thought that maybe if I showed him some trust and goodwill, he'd see that he could have them anytime he wanted to, and he'd ease up on his demands for custody. But I hadn't let him go without some guarantees. Before leaving, he'd signed notarized statements promising to return the children by 6 P.M. the following Sunday. The statement spelled out flight numbers, and hotel names and included his written promise to have the children call me every night they were away.

The day they'd left, Jane had stood by Federico's car crying, her thin shoulders hunched.

"I don't want to go," she had sobbed. Her green eyes, so like mine, pleaded with me. "Mommy, don't make me go. I want to stay with you."

I tried to reassure her. She would have lots of fun. I would talk to her every night and she'd be back home in just a few days. I had felt responsible for her fearfulness. One night, weeks before that, I had started to cry in front of her. She'd never seen that before. When she asked what was wrong, I'd blurted out that I was afraid her daddy would take her and Michael away from me and never bring them back. I'd regretted that outburst many times, because it had planted the same fear in her. Several times when Federico had come to pick the children up for the weekend, she had begged me to tell him she didn't want to go, and I'd say that she had to tell him herself. But she couldn't bring herself to disappoint him. I sometimes worried that she was too obedient, too eager to please.

All that week they were in Miami, I felt uneasy. Had I been foolish? After all, it was the perfect opportunity for Federico to take off for Bolivia with the children and never come back. Each night I'd be relieved by the sound of their chirping voices over the phone. When he came back with them a week later I nearly wept with relief—relief that they were home and, even more important, relief that I'd never have to worry about Federico kidnapping them again. If he hadn't done it this time, I thought, then he never would.

But now I wasn't so sure. He was two hours late. By eight o'clock I had called every friend of his I could think of. No one had seen him. By nine o'clock I knew something was very wrong. I called my lawyer at home. He was surprised to hear from me on a Sunday night.

"Is anything wrong?"

"He hasn't brought the kids back yet. I'm worried."

Mr. Rosenthal's voice was calm but concerned. "Have you called every place where they might be?" Yes, I had. "Don't panic. Just hang tight. Wait until ten o'clock, and if he hasn't brought them back by then, call me."

I hung up the phone. As I waited, my stomach slowly squeezed itself into an icy ball. The minutes crawled by. Finally it was ten o'clock. Hand shaking,

I dialed Mr. Rosenthal's number again. "They're still not back." My voice sounded high pitched and childish.

"Okay. I'm coming over right now."

I waited outside in the parking lot. It wasn't cold but my teeth began to chatter uncontrollably. In a few minutes he pulled up. I slid into the front seat and immediately felt reassured just being in his presence.

Mr. Rosenthal was a bundle of contradictions. He came across as a good ol' boy, yet he was Jewish. Born and raised in the tiny South Texas town of Three Rivers, he'd become one of the most respected civil attorneys in the state. He was a member of the highly esteemed American College of Trial Lawyers. He was brash and outspoken, yet there was another side to him that was soft and kind.

For the past five months he had been not only my lawyer and adviser, but also my friend.

Yet in spite of our closeness, I never called him Douglas. He was always "Mr. Rosenthal" to me. I don't know why exactly. Maybe it was out of respect for his position as senior partner at Patton & Jones, the law firm where I worked as a legal assistant, or because he was seventeen years older than I was. He teased me about it often and asked me to call him by his first name, but it just didn't seem right to me.

Mr. Rosenthal didn't normally handle divorces, but at the request of Kathy Rupard, his secretary and my friend, he had taken my case. I knew my case was small potatoes compared to the multimillion-dollar lawsuits he usually handled. And I was acutely aware that my simple divorce had turned into a messy custody battle and a colossal pain in the neck. But he had never made me feel like an imposition. In fact he seemed to welcome my visits to his office. His eyes twinkling beneath bushy eyebrows, cigar clenched in his teeth, he had a way of making an irreverent comment that cut straight to the heart of a matter. He cajoled me out of the dumps; he forced me to see things in perspective; he made me laugh about things that weren't laughable.

But tonight his impish grin was absent, his mouth under the iron gray mustache unsmiling.

First we drove across town to Federico's apartment complex and circled the parking lot. His car wasn't there. I didn't know which apartment was his, so we couldn't investigate on our own. Next we drove to the police station. He explained the situation to the officer at the front desk, who promised to send a patrolman to check out Federico's apartment. They'd call us as soon as they knew something. We drove to the law offices to wait for news. It was after midnight.

In Mr. Rosenthal's modern chrome and leather office, I sat across from him as I had many times before. He leaned back in his chair, his feet on the desk, and took out a cigar. It was a familiar scene, except that instead of a tailor-made suit and Gucci shoes he was wearing a Mexican *guayabera* shirt, shorts, and sneakers. And instead of the constant interruption of his telephone, the office was eerily quiet. We were both unusually silent, too.

Then he produced a deck of cards and we started to play gin rummy, but without much enthusiasm. The clock on his wall was ticking loudly.

16

"I wonder when that policeman is going to call," I finally said.

"We should be hearing something pretty soon," he said, shifting the cigar in his mouth and laying down some cards

"He promised me. He promised me he'd never do this," I thought aloud. I remembered the scene clearly. One week after Federico had moved out of our apartment and filed for divorce, he had sat across from me at the kitchen table, begging me to let him have one of the children. "Please, just give one to me and you can keep the other. We could live with my mother in La Paz." Like the story of King Solomon and the baby. I couldn't bear the thought of it.

No, I had said. No.

Then for the first time a monstrous fear rose up in my mind. What if he decided to take one of them anyway, or even both? I would be helpless to stop him. He had a legal right to see them. What if some afternoon when he took them for an outing he didn't come back?

"Please don't ever take them away from me," I had begged, and started to cry. Federico knew that I didn't cry easily, and the tears took him by surprise. For a moment the hard look on his face softened. "I wouldn't do that to the kids. I know what it was like for you, growing up without a mother. I wouldn't do that to them."

"Promise me. Promise you never will."

"I promise," he had said.

Now, back in the law office, I said, "After he brought them back from Miami last summer, I thought I could trust him."

Mr. Rosenthal's eyes were cynical as he looked up from his cards. He could have said, "I told you so," but wisely didn't. How many times had I heard him mutter that he didn't trust the "slimy bastard"? Instead, he said patiently, "You don't *know* for a fact that he's taken them. Maybe he went to visit somebody out of town, in Harlingen or Brownsville or somewhere, and couldn't get back."

He went on with a few other possible explanations, but I was only half listening. Did he really believe any of it? I studied him. Undisciplined salt-and-pepper curls framed his broad face. His nose had been broken and reconstructed so many times—the first time after a childhood accident—that he now had the look of a boxer who'd been in the ring too long.

His thick eyebrows were drawn together and he wore a look of concerned reassurance. But I could tell that he was hiding something from me now. Could it be that he was as worried as I was? But, so desperately did I want to believe him that I seized on his reassuring words. We turned back to the card game. I struggled to concentrate, but the cards in my hands became a jumble of numbers and colors. The clock ticked on.

Finally, around 2 A.M., the phone jangled. Mr. Rosenthal answered it. His face began to tighten as he listened, and the ball of ice in my stomach turned to lead. "Uh-huh . . . uh-huh . . . nothing, huh? Well, you have my number. If y'all find out anything, let me know." He hung up and looked at me with baleful eyes.

18

"That was the police officer they sent out to check on Freddy's apartment. He said the door was open, and everything had been cleaned out—clothes, dishes, everything."

"Everything?" I echoed.

He nodded.

I had been steeling myself for this news for hours; I'd even been expecting it. But his words skimmed across my consciousness like rocks skipping water. I covered my face with my hands, not to cry, but to shut out the room and force the meaning of his words into my brain. Why didn't I scream, why didn't I beat the walls with my fists? Instead I felt hollow, stunned, frozen in time and space, as if a balloon inside me had popped and everything had collapsed in on itself. Mr. Rosenthal knelt in front of me and patted me awkwardly on the back.

He was saying something. "The police have a description of his car and the license plate number. They'll be looking for him."

My babies are gone.

"First thing in the morning we'll get a court order to stop him from leaving the country."

"It's too late," I whispered through my hands.

My babies are gone.

"You don't know that," he said, but without much conviction. "Let me call Susan and have her come stay with you tonight. You shouldn't be by yourself."

"No, I'll be all right." How calm I sounded. How could that be?

Mr. Rosenthal argued with me briefly but gave up without his usual spunk. For once he had no ready answer, no advice, no funny stories to tell. He drove me home through the silent deserted streets.

Once in the apartment I went straight to Jane and Michael's room. Everything tonight had seemed so unreal. Maybe it had all been a weird dream and I would find them sleeping soundly in their beds. I hesitated a moment and then switched on the light. A self-portrait of Jane in her Supergirl costume grinned crookedly down at me from the wall. A brace of toy dinosaurs stood frozen in combat on the floor. I turned to look at their beds. They were rumpled and unmade . . . and empty. I buried my face in Michael's pillow, where his scent still lingered. It was no dream. There would be no last-minute reprieve from this nightmare.

Chapter Two

Monday, November 16, 1987

The next morning, as promised, Mr. Rosenthal picked me up at eight to go to the courthouse. It was in the county seat, a small town about fifteen miles north of McAllen. On the way we passed fragrant groves of oranges. The December harvest was only a month away, and the trees were heavy with fruit. Palm trees lined the road, their leafy tops swaying in the breeze. It seemed incredible that the world around me was as beautiful as before. I felt strangely removed from it, as if I were looking at it through an invisible curtain.

At the courthouse Mr. Rosenthal and I went to the District Attorney's office, where we were ushered into the office of a young assistant D.A., Omar Trevino. His desk was cluttered with files, and he looked harassed and overworked. He stood up and extended his hand.

"How can I help you?"

Mr. Rosenthal introduced me and told Mr.

Trevino briefly what had happened the night before.

"We want to stop Mr. Bascope from leaving the country with those children. I'm not familiar with criminal law so I have no idea what we have to do to accomplish that."

Mr. Trevino sat back down and motioned for us to take a seat. "Hmm, I've never run into a case like this before. But I know that you'll need court orders—probably a writ of habeas corpus and a warrant for his arrest from the sheriff's office." He shook his head. "But I don't know if there's any way to stop him if he's already left the jurisdiction of this court."

My heart sank. That meant that if he was already out of Hidalgo County—which he surely was—he was out of reach.

Mr. Trevino began to leaf through a law book. I sat perched on the edge of a wooden chair, suppressing the urge to scream, "Hurry up! Every second counts!" Maybe there was still time to stop them. Maybe at this moment they were at an airport, waiting for the plane that would take them away forever.

Trevino put down the book. "If he's already left Texas, you're gonna have to get the Feds involved in it. I know a guy in the FBI office in McAllen. I can call him and see what you have to do to get a federal warrant issued." As he was making the call, a secretary stepped into the doorway.

"There's a phone call for Mr. Rosenthal." He went to a desk outside Mr. Trevino's office to take the call and returned a few minutes later.

"That was my secretary." It looks like Bascope might still be in the country. She called the Carter Apparel Company—that's where he was working—and they said he'd called in this morning to ask for a 'personal day' off."

My pulse quickened. They *must* still be in the country . . . but why would he call in to work if he was planning to disappear? It didn't make sense.

"Where was he calling from? What did he say?" I asked.

"I don't know. Kathy just talked to the receptionist there. The plant manager was in a meeting, but he's supposed to call me as soon as he gets out."

Meanwhile, Trevino had talked to his friend at the FBI. "To stop this guy from leaving the country you need a *federal* indictment, not just a state one."

"What do we have to do to get that?" Mr. Rosenthal asked.

"Well, first you'll need the judge who has jurisdiction over the divorce case to sign several different court orders. Then you take those to the sheriff's department and they'll issue a warrant for his arrest. Only after that warrant is issued can you get the federal indictment." He went on explaining the process. I felt more and more frustrated as I listened. What he was talking about would take days.

The secretary announced another phone call for Mr. Rosenthal. This time I followed him into the next room. After listening a moment, he began to frown. "I see, so there wasn't any phone call. Uh-huh . . . Yes. Well, I appreciate your calling. And please call my office if you hear anything."

He hung up and looked at me. "That was the plant manager at Carter's. Freddy never called there this morning. That was just a story they were giving out—at his request. In fact, he got fired a month ago. The plant manager hasn't seen him since he came in to pick up his check several weeks ago."

Fired a month ago? My throat went dry. "Then why . . . ?"

"They were covering for him in case the social worker called to check on his job status. Federico didn't want him to know he'd been fired." He added dryly, "I guess he thought it might hurt his chances for getting custody."

The court had appointed a social worker to evaluate the two homes, Federico's and mine, and to recommend to the judge which was better for the children. He had recommended mine.

"When this guy got Kathy's message this morning and found out that Freddy had taken off with the kids, he thought he'd better call me and tell me the truth."

I was blinded by tears of frustration and anger—frustration at having my hopes raised and then dashed, anger at Federico's deception, and at his boss for helping him with it. If only I'd known he was out of a job . . . I'd never have let the kids out of my sight, even if it meant camping on his doorstep every other weekend. And how cool he'd been. Even after he'd been fired, he'd come to pick them up dressed in slacks and a tie, as if he were on his way home from work.

In spite of my anger, I felt a stab of pity for him.

He must have felt desperate after he'd lost this job—his second since we'd come back to the United States two years ago. I remembered how hard those first seven months in Austin had been, his grueling search for a job and the toll it had taken on him. He couldn't have done it again. And—my anger surged up again—he would have been too proud to slink home to Bolivia empty-handed. So he'd taken the children.

None of that mattered now. He was surely well on his way to Bolivia, if he hadn't already arrived. Mr. Rosenthal must have read this thought in my eyes. He said gently, "Cass, he might not be out of reach yet. We'll go back to my office and get Kathy to type up those court orders right away. Then we'll come back this afternoon and get Judge Villarreal to sign them. There's still hope."

While we were at the courthouse, Kathy had been busy herself. Kathy, who was from my native West Texas, was an attractive mother of two, happily married to her high school sweetheart, and a woman of unyielding convictions. Not only had she called Federico's former boss, she had also phoned his former landlady, who'd told her that yes, Mr. Bascope had moved out of his apartment the previous Saturday. In fact, he'd given two months' notice of his intentions to leave. No, he hadn't left a forwarding address. The landlady also mentioned having seen an Asian man who was helping Mr. Bascope move.

"I know who the Asian must be," I told Mr. Rosenthal when he returned to the car where I sat waiting. Wan was a Korean who ran a small electronics shop in downtown McAllen, one of dozens of such shops that did most of their business with Mexicans from across the border, only eight miles away. We had bought a television set from him when we'd first moved to McAllen, and Federico, in typical fashion—in Bolivia you had to bargain and haggle before buying anything, so it was an advantage to befriend the seller—had ingratiated himself with Wan. When Federico and I had separated, Wan had helped him move out of our apartment. He owned a large van that came in handy on such occasions. I was fairly sure that Wan was the same Asian the landlady had seen.

Mr. Rosenthal and I drove to his shop, one of many similar establishments lining the street. As soon as Wan saw me, his face took on a guarded expression. He gave me a curt nod. Mr. Rosenthal handed him one of his business cards.

"I'm Doug Rosenthal, Mrs. Bascope's attorney. We'd like to talk with you if you have a few minutes." Wan led us past stacks of television sets and stereos to his cluttered office at the back of the shop. There he sat behind his desk and motioned for us to take a seat. Mr. Rosenthal remained standing, one foot propped on an empty TV box. He glanced at Wan's business card.

"Mr. Ho," he began, "I represent Mrs. Bascope in the divorce between her and Mr. Bascope. It seems that Mr. Bascope has disappeared and taken her children with him. We were just wondering if you might know something about where he's gone."

Wan's face remained expressionless as he listened, nervously tapping a pencil on his desk. He claimed to know nothing. But when Mr. Rosenthal told him that Federico's landlady had seen him helping Federico move out of his apartment on Saturday, Wan admitted, "Yes, I helped him." He added quickly, "But I don't know where he was planning to go."

"You mean he didn't even mention where he was moving to?"

"He didn't tell me anything. He just say he was moving."

"Well, was he planning to *drive* there?"

"No."

"How do you know that?"

"He sold me his car."

"Didn't you wonder what kind of place he was going where he wouldn't need a car?"

"No. He sold it to me for very good price. I didn't ask questions." Wan was getting increasingly nervous.

"What else did you buy from him?"

"I bought nothing else from him. We make a trade, though. He came into my shop early last week because he wanted to trade his VCR."

"What did he want to trade it for?" I asked quickly.

"He had a VHS-type VCR and he wanted to trade it for a Betamax."

For me, that clinched it. I turned to Mr. Rosenthal.

27

"In Bolivia they use only Betamax. I know that's where he's gone."

Mr. Rosenthal asked Wan if he knew that I had legal custody of the children and that Federico had broken the law by taking them. He hinted that Wan might be considered an accomplice, but Wan kept repeating that he didn't know anything. It was clear he wasn't going to reveal anything else. He was visibly relieved when he walked us to the front of the store and saw us out.

Inside the car, Mr. Rosenthal muttered, "That lying little weasel. He probably drove them to the airport himself."

"It doesn't matter," I said. "They're long gone."

That afternooon we returned to the courthouse. Judge Villarreal grimly signed every document put in front of him: writs of habeas corpus, demands to return the children to the custody of the court, orders finding Federico in contempt, orders for his arrest. Federico's lawyer showed up only long enough to present his motion to withdraw from the case. He had little to say about what Federico had done, except, of course, that he didn't know anything about it.

Armed with the signed court orders, we went to the sheriff's office. We talked to a burly female investigator named Lisa Murillo and wrote affidavits setting out the events of Sunday night and our reasons for believing that Federico had kidnapped the children. This was the first step in getting a warrant issued and a stop order sent to all international airports and other ports of exit.

Sometime that afternoon, I telephoned my father in Austin. As soon as I heard his voice, the dam burst and I began to bawl like a baby. "Daddy," I sobbed, "Federico took Jane and Michael."

There was stunned silence for a moment. Then he asked, "Where are they?"

"I think they're in Bolivia."

He said quietly, "I'm so sorry, darling." At that point there wasn't much comfort he could offer, but I knew he was hurting for me as only a parent can.

I dug old photograph albums out of boxes the next morning and spread them around me on the floor. The sheriff's office needed pictures of Federico and the children for identification. I picked up one of the albums and began to turn the pages. It was hard to believe that these photographs were all that was left of our marriage. I stared at a picture of Federico as he was when I'd first met him. He was leaning forward earnestly, dark hair curling around his ears, and in the lamplight his eyes were startlingly clear and intense.

Chapter Three

Austin, Texas, 1975

It was the summer of 1975 at the University of Texas. Federico was working on his master's degree in economics, and I was getting mine in English. I was the girl from the flat West Texas plains who'd always yearned to travel, to roam the English moors of the Brontë novels, to float down the Amazon River, to safari across the African savannah—the more exotic the better. The more different from my background other places and people were, the more fascinating I found them. So it wasn't surprising that Federico intrigued me, with his Latin good looks, his accent, and what I imagined to be a suave international air.

We met quite by accident. In the summer session of that year we both decided to take a course just for fun: beginning French. It was the first day of class. The students' chatter died away as a large woman strode into the room, dumped some books on the desk, and sang out in a lilting accent,

"Bonjour, mes étudiantes. Comment allez-vous?" We all looked at each other in puzzled delight. Mademoiselle St. Clair, who in spite of her name was a homespun Texan like most of the rest of us, had a pixieish sense of fun that set the tone for the rest of the semester.

That first day, when she commanded us to introduce ourselves in French, my attention zeroed in on the foreign student in the front row, the older one with the serious expression and aquiline nose. He seemed mature, wise, self-contained, even a little aloof. His name was Federico, but he was soon rechristened Frederique. I was Catherine, pronounced the French way: Cat-er-een.

From that day I began to subtly pursue Frederique. After class he'd always pick up a copy of the campus newspaper at a kiosk just outside the building. I would "happen" to be there at the same time. We'd exchange a few pleasantries and then go our separate ways. He seemed unfailingly polite, and even gallant in an old-world way—or maybe I'd read too many English novels. He had a vague and distracted air about him and didn't seem interested in me. Rather than discourage me, this only spurred me on. One day he walked me to my dorm, wheeling his ten-speed bike alongside. A few days later, he asked me to dinner. We began seeing each other.

I learned that he had grown up in Bolivia in a rather privileged family. His European ancestry automatically placed him among the white-skinned upper classes. His mother's family hailed from the Andalusian region of Spain, and his father's ancestors had been Basques from France. His father had died when Federico was a toddler, he told me, and his stepfather, now a doctor with the United Nations, had emigrated to Bolivia after fleeing Nazi Germany.

I was impressed with Federico's stories of growing up in houses full of servants, with chauffeurs to drive the family's Mercedes-Benz. He had traveled all over South America and Europe, he told me. He described his childhood in Tarija, a lovely town in the south of Bolivia, close to the border of Argentina, where grape vineyards covered the hillsides, women wore flowers tucked behind their ears, and natives spoke in the lilting dialect used in the days of Cervantes. It was all very charming.

While he was a university student in Bolivia, Federico met an American girl, a Peace Corps volunteer. They fell in love. When her stint with the Peace Corps was over, Federico returned with her to Texas and they were married. He studied English while she got her master's degree in social work from the University of Texas at Austin. Now, three years later, he told me they were divorced. He was staying in Austin long enough to finish his master's degree in economics and was putting himself through school by waiting tables in a Mexican restaurant.

It wasn't until we'd been seeing each other for

several months that I learned that Federico wasn't divorced after all. At first I was furious. But by then I was in love, and it didn't take long for me to accept his explanation. He had told me that he was *getting* a divorce, not that he already had one; I had simply misunderstood. It seemed plausible enough—communication was never easy between us. And a few months after our near breakup, he was indeed divorced. So began a rather rocky relationship that continued for the next three years.

Early in the summer of 1978, Federico's stepfather died. His newly widowed mother needed him. He decided to return to Bolivia as soon as the fall semester ended.

For the first time in our relationship we discussed marriage. It was under the pressure of imminent separation that we made wedding plans. With some misgivings on my part (but doesn't everyone have the jitters?) we were married in November of 1978. Two weeks later we arrived in La Paz, Bolivia.

My dream of traveling to foreign lands had come true—but Bolivia didn't exactly match my dreams. I was suddenly catapulted into a world different from any I had ever known or imagined. Sure, Federico had told me about the snow-capped mountains and the colorful Indians, but he hadn't told me that everywhere, all the time, inside or out, it was cold in La Paz, and there was no such thing as indoor heating. He hadn't told me that we'd be stuck in a cramped, cheerless apartment with his mother Nila for nine months. He hadn't told me that almost everything I ate and drank during the first year would give me the Inca equivalent of Montezuma's revenge, until my stomach incubated its own colony of hardy native amoebas. And he hadn't told me that instead of welcoming me into the family, my new in-laws would all but ignore me.

At that point I couldn't speak any Spanish and with the exception of Federico's sister Ana Maria, they couldn't speak English. Every Sunday the family would gather for a huge midday meal in Nila's apartment. In front of us all, Nila would scold Federico for marrying a useless American woman who didn't know how to cook or do anything else a wife was supposed to do. What good was my college degree? What did a woman need that for? Why hadn't he married a nice girl from his hometown? To his credit, Federico defended me as I sat picking at my food.

It was worse during the day, when Federico left for his job as an assistant at an import firm. Nila was nothing if not energetic. She furiously dusted, swept, and cooked all morning long. When I pitched in to help, she'd scold me for doing it all wrong, but if I didn't offer to help, she'd scold me for my laziness. Nila and I had a few screaming matches; she would shout at me in Spanish, which I barely understood, and I would shout back at her in English, which she understood not at all.

Sometimes we'd shout at the same time—after all, it didn't matter if either of us actually *heard* what the other was saying. It was only later that I could see the humor in these scenes.

In La Paz I saw no trace of the lifestyle Federico had described to me. There were no servants or fine cars with chauffeurs. When her husband died, Nila's standard of living fell drastically. She had to move out of their spacious apartment suite and rent it as office space. With the rental proceeds and her UN widow's pension she was buying another large condominium, but in the interim she lived meanly in the apartment we shared with her, which was about as cozy as a cave.

After nine miserable months, Nila traveled to West Berlin to visit one of her sons. On the eve of her departure, she held a going-away tea in her apartment. Even though I lived there, she pointedly neglected to invite me. I stayed in my room, listening to the clinking cups and laughter of Nila and her friends.

While Nila was in Berlin, Federico and I moved into our own apartment. For me, life improved dramatically. I got a job in the evenings teaching English at a small business college. Later, I taught English to overprivileged ninth, tenth, and twelfth graders, both American and foreign, at the private American school in La Paz. Meanwhile, Federico had become the assistant manager of a textile factory. We still spent a lot of time with my in-laws, but by then I could speak decent Spanish, and the gatherings were more enjoyable. Nila and I got along better after her return from Germany.

Federico's older brother Rene, an electrician, was forty years old and never married. He was shy, nervous, and intense, yet kind. Rene and Federico were Nila's children from her first husband. When Federico was still a toddler, she had married Dr. Kann and had had three more children: Edgar, Manuel and Ana Maria.

Edgar and Manuel attended the University of Berlin and stayed in West Berlin after their graduation. Edgar was a mining engineer. He was unmarried but living with a German girl and their small daughter. Manuel was a clinical psychologist. He was married to a Peruvian woman and they had two sons.

The youngest of Federico's siblings, and the only girl, was Ana Maria. Pretty and spoiled, Ana Maria was the only one of the children who lived with her parents during the years Dr. Kann was stationed in UN posts in Burma and Afghanistan. She had been educated in private American schools and had traveled all over Europe. Beside Spanish, she spoke fluent English, German, and Farsi. She was married to a dentist, Horacio, from Buenos Aires, and they lived in La Paz with their two children. On the eve of the birth of their son, Edgar married his German girlfriend and they moved to La Paz. After a few years, Rene finally got married to Lily, a hairdresser.

We spent time together endlessly, and I got to know my in-laws very well. Lily and Rene were always kind and generous. Rene was always running errands for his mother, and Lily spent a lot of time giving free haircuts and perms to the other women in the family. Edgar had been a radical student in Spain in the movement against Franco and had even spent time in jail there as a result of his involvement. He was still a revolutionary at heart and seemed to have genuine concern for the downtrodden. For now, though, his main concern was providing for his unhappy wife and their children. He wore a constant look of worry, and his German wife Monika lived in frustration at the difficulties of living in Bolivia and trying to learn Spanish. She and I probably would have been better friends if we'd had a language in common.

Ana Maria and Horacio were caught up in the social whirl of the German and Argentine Embassies. They entertained often, and their main interest was to accumulate fine and costly possessions. They could talk of little else. Horacio was a walking encyclopedia of the best brands of any product you could name, but his snobbishness annoyed me less than his habit of making jokes about my height. I towered head and shoulders above everyone in the family except Federico, and Horacio's teasing wore thin. These made up the clan, the hub around which our lives revolved for six and a half years.

I was learning what it meant to be a housewife

in Bolivia. I learned the art of haggling with surly Indian vendors in the marketplaces. I learned how to take a twenty-pound chunk of raw meat and cut it into manageable pieces. Cooking was time consuming and labor intensive. Preparing the noon meal was the task of an entire morning. Frozen or packaged foods were nonexistent, and canned food was expensive and of inferior quality. There were peas to shell, and meat to cut and pound into tenderness. Tap water wasn't potable, so each day one had to boil a tub of water and then allow it to cool for drinking. Raw fruits and vegetables had to be soaked in iodine to kill harmful bacteria (farmers fertilized their fields with their own waste). There was an unwritten rule that lunch had to begin with homemade soup. This was made with stock from boiling either beef bones, or from boiling the inedible parts of a chicken: the head and the feet. I remember the first time I lifted the lid off a boiling pot in my mother-in-law's kitchen only to find the glazed eye of a chicken staring up at me, and chicken claws bobbling around in the stock. The main course was a meat dish, served up with several vegetable dishes and the obligatory rice and boiled potatoes. Dessert was fresh fruit, followed by coffee or coca tea, made from boiled leaves from the coca plant. It was an enormous amount of food.

Breakfast was light, continental style, with bread and coffee, and instead of supper there was late-afternoon tea, which consisted of more bread and coffee or tea.

Washing clothes was quite a project. There were no laundromats, and a personally owned washer or dryer was an unheard-of luxury. Every house and apartment came equipped with its own laundry room: a tiny cement cubicle with a built-in washtub. Maids would stand at the washtub, rubbing and wringing the clothes by hand. The only "detergent" on the market was a harsh soap powder that was used for everything from washing dishes to scrubbing toilets. Washed clothes were hung to dry on lines strung across the laundry room.

Maids did the ironing, too—and did they ever. I couldn't convince them that it wasn't necessary to iron *everything*. Bras, men's underwear, and washcloths did quite nicely without being ironed. Over the years I threw away many a dainty thing that had been scorched with a hot iron.

Items I had always considered necessities—breakfast cereal, underarm deodorant, paper towels, and later, baby food and disposable diapers—were either unavailable or prohibitively expensive. I learned to do without or to make my own. No mayonnaise? No problem. I made it at home in a blender. No baby food? I made that at home too. I learned from the Bolivians, who were wonderfully inventive at finding unusual uses for ordinary items. If what they needed wasn't at hand, they'd adapt something else to do the job.

I learned about dealing with maids, although with limited success. When we first moved to Bolivia, I was amused at the women's constant complaints about the "servant problem"—that is, until I had maids of my own. They were either sullen and argumentative or jolly and irresponsible, sure to disappear during the next fiesta day.

But because of the lack of labor-saving devices, maids were almost a necessity. There were hardwood floors to sweep and polish, clothes to wash by hand, rugs to beat. Maids were also incredibly inexpensive—it cost the equivalent of $20 a month for a full-time, live-in housekeeper.

Eventually I made friends with other Americans in the community. Most were with the U.S. Embassy, or the U.S. Agency for International Development, or one of the various church missions. For a while my only social life outside of Federico's family consisted in attending *gringa* teas held by American wives married to Bolivian husbands. But I didn't go for long. The teas were an excuse for wives to get together and complain about Bolivia and everything in it, and by then I was beginning to find the country fascinating.

Physically, Bolivia was a land of contrasts. La Paz was on the flat high plains between the eastern and western ranges of the Andes mountains. It was two miles above sea level and chilly year round. But you could hop in your car and in two hours be in the steamy Zongo Valley, where oranges grew wild and parrots squawked in the trees.

The road leading from La Paz to the Zongo twisted tortuously from the icy heights of the Andean peaks into an emerald valley nestled between steep mountainsides. The first time we rounded a bend and I saw the mist rising up from the Zongo, it was like seeing the Hudson River painting "Heart of the Andes" come to life. The warm, moist breeze of the Zongo felt like a caress against my skin, so different from the cold, dry air of La Paz.

Two hours away from La Paz to the East lay another jungle valley with an equally exotic name, the Yungas. There the towns' Indian names rolled off the tongue like strange music: Chulumani, Unduavi, Socabaya. We once stayed in the Yungas in a hillside hotel nestled among orange and coffee trees and surrounded by coca fields. (Even though its leaves are used to make cocaine, coca is grown legally in Bolivia. Indians for centuries have chewed its leaves to alleviate fatigue and hunger. The tea brewed from its leaves was served universally in private homes and restaurants alike.) In the Yungas, we picked wild oranges—enough to fill the trunk of the car—and took them back to La Paz to distribute among the family.

Bolivia was full of other kinds of contrasts, too: rich and poor, beautiful and ugly, kind and mean spirited. I had never seen so many Mercedes-Benz automobiles in one place, yet the vast majority of people had no car at all and got around on crowded, smelly buses. Beautiful mansions surrounded by well-manicured gardens could be found on the same street as mud shacks with half-naked children playing in the doorways.

People who didn't know you could be insufferably rude. Customers were all but ignored by store clerks and marketplace vendors, who didn't seem to care one whit whether you bought from them or not. But people who knew you were effusively warm and affectionate. It was the custom to greet anyone you had even a passing acquaintance with, male or female, with a kiss on both cheeks. It took me a while to get the hang of knowing which cheek to aim for first and to master the art of brushing the air with my lips without actually touching skin.

There were other customs to get used to: the way Bolivians made promises and arranged vague social dates they had no intention of keeping, the eight o'clock dinner invitation that really meant ten-thirty, the fact that there was only one correct way to do everything—the Bolivian way.

There was a yawning gap between the sexes, with rigidly defined roles and expectations. At parties everyone separated immediately into two groups: men and women. I soon learned that the men expected to be left alone by the women, except when the women served them. Each woman would heap a plate with the choicest bits of food and then serve it to her husband. Then women and children would eat what was left. The women sat on one side of the room and discussed maids, children, and manicures, and the men swigged beer on the other side of the room and discussed politics.

Once, before I understood the rules, I got bored with the women's corner and ventured onto the men's side of the room to stand at Federico's elbow. The men's discussion faltered and an embarrassed hush fell over them as they wondered what to do about me. I slunk off to join the women again.

Federico and I had our own share of problems. Almost from the moment we got married, his ardor for me seemed to cool. I was puzzled and hurt, but he denied that anything was different. In many other little ways he became less attentive. It was as if from the moment we were married he thought, "I have her now; I'll turn my attention to other things."

And there were plenty of other things he could turn his attention to. In Austin he had been just one of the faceless crowd. In Bolivia, he was *somebody*. In Bolivia he was in his element, on his old stomping grounds. In Tarija he'd played on the national basketball team, and many people still remembered him as a sports star.

In his new job he was important, too. As manager of a large textile plant, he was master of the fate of some three hundred workers. Fresh out of an American college and bursting with new ideas, he had set about modernizing the plant and introducing new management techniques. He renewed

43

friendships with old high school buddies and every week played soccer or basketball with them. Later, he became president of Bolivia's National Basketball Association and was caught up in planning the South American Championship games, which he arranged to have in Tarija. He was often in the papers and on the news. I was glad for him and proud of his accomplishments. But few of his activities included me, and I began to feel like nothing more than a cheerleader on the sidelines.

I was homesick. I missed Daddy, the hum of the air conditioner on a hot day, my tropical fish. I craved baked potatoes with sour cream, a breakfast of Grape Nuts, and an occasional enchilada. I missed Texas and all things Texan. I even missed country music, and I'd never even liked it before then. I put a travel book about Texas on our coffee table, eager to talk about home, but nobody ever asked. Bolivians were strangely insulated, so preoccupied with their own country and its overwhelming problems that they never asked me what it was like in my country. Besides, they thought they knew all about it from the movies.

Federico had no patience with my problems in adapting. In fact, talking about any problem was out of the question. He had a way of denying anything unpleasant as if it simply didn't exist. If he didn't like the truth, he simply made up his own truth and seemed to believe it himself. I suppose that was why he'd lied about his father. His father hadn't died; he'd deserted Nila when Federico and Rene were toddlers. He was alive and well and living in Cochabamba, Bolivia. I learned this quite by accident from one of Federico's cousins. When I asked Federico why he hadn't told me the truth, he simply shrugged. Another pointless lie came to light: Far from being a cosmopolitan world traveler, he'd never even been to Europe.

Even though he took pride in what he considered his "modern" attitudes about women, I felt that I was a disappointment to him in ways that mattered in his society. Wives in Bolivia were judged largely by their culinary skills. Every day Nila served up enormous and delicious meals. She was known for her excellent cooking. I was only an average cook by American standards and woefully inadequate by Bolivian standards. Federico picked at the food I placed before him, yet at his mother's house he stuffed himself to the point of being sick. Although his family was polite when we invited them to dinner, it was obvious that they considered American dishes to be substandard and my attempts at Bolivian cooking were even worse.

Federico's family were always arguing. There'd be shouting and then a few minutes later it was as if nothing had happened. Federico took to shouting at me, even in public. This infuriated me. I took to turning on my heel and walking away when he did it. In my family we *never* shouted.

But eventually the challenges of surviving in a country in constant turmoil overshadowed any problems in our marriage.

One of the bloodiest coups d'etat took place during our second year in La Paz. Army troops led by General Busch stormed the presidential palace and took over the Presidency. The elected president fled and went into hiding. A state of siege was declared. Curfew was at sunset; after that one could be shot on sight. Someone from the U.S. Embassy called to advise us to lie low for a few days. There were no flights into or out of the country, and disgruntled tourists were stranded for days in hotels in the city. There was no phone communication to the exterior, newspapers were banned, and the only news available was radio propaganda put out by the new military government.

Those who had short-wave radios could find out what was really happening by listening to the Voice of America. The rest of us could only watch the tanks as they rumbled up the street and listen to the sounds of grenades and gunfire coming from downtown. Federico and I ventured outside only to make runs to the neighborhood store for bread and canned goods, since no fresh food or milk was being brought into town. Nervous young soldiers with automatic weapons stood on every street corner. The U.S. Embassy called a meeting at the American school to discuss evacuation plans, should they become necessary. After a few days, the new military junta surrendered against overwhelming opposition, but not until many people had lost their lives—mostly Bolivian citizens who, protesting in the streets by shouting and throwing rocks, were mowed down by tanks.

Along with the political turmoil there was economic instability, which eventually led to chaos. The Bolivian peso was holding steady at 25 pesos to the dollar when we arrived in 1978, but by the time we left in 1985 the exchange rate was more than a million to one. Bolivia had the dubious distinction of having the highest inflation rate— 36,000 percent—in the world. Merchants hoarded their products and refused to sell, knowing that if they waited a day or even an hour longer, prices would be even higher. Bus and taxi drivers would go on strike, demanding higher fares, and when that happened everything shut down. One day I was stranded downtown several miles from home when transportation workers announced a strike. I started walking. Even though I took off my boots after a couple of miles and trudged the rest of the way home in stockinged feet, by the time I arrived my feet were swollen to twice their size. I learned quickly that in Bolivia, politics wasn't just something you read about in the paper.

Chapter Four

Amid the social and political turmoil something more personal happened to distract me: I became pregnant in the spring of 1980. Almost as soon as I got the positive test results from the lab, I had a miscarriage. I was crushed. But a few months later I was pregnant again. My in-laws were ecstatic. I was finally going to do something worthwhile: I would have Federico's baby. I was the typical glowing mother-to-be. Except for some morning sickness during the first trimester, my pregnancy was problem-free. I was proud of my growing belly.

I kept my job teaching English at the Bank of America until the Christmas break. Then, during long afternoons at home, I taught myself to crochet and made little blankets out of granny squares. My proudest creation was a white doll-sized blanket with tiny satin ribbons woven through it. Then I ambitiously crocheted a cap to match. It came out impossibly small—it would've fit snugly over a large orange—and everyone who saw it laughed and said it would be much too little for the baby.

I faithfully kept my doctor's appointments and followed his advice to the letter: no drinking, no smoking, no salt, plenty of vitamins. But during the last two months of my pregnancy, sonograms showed that the baby had nearly stopped growing. Neither the pediatrician nor the obstetrician knew why. Maybe it was because the oxygen was very thin in La Paz, because of the altitude, and I wasn't getting enough oxygen to the baby. Maybe the placenta was too small. Anyway, they decided that as soon as the baby was due, it should be born—it was just too dangerous for it to remain inside.

So on a Friday night, April 10, 1981, Federico drove me to the hospital. I was hooked up to an intravenous drip to induce labor. By Saturday night I had been in labor all day and my water had burst, but there was still no dilation. My doctor frowned and shook his head, but said we would wait a while longer. By Sunday at noon, I had not eaten for two days and had been in labor for a day and a half. Dr. Teran announced that we couldn't wait any longer. I'd have to undergo a C-section.

"All those wasted Lamaze classes!" I moaned. I squeezed Federico's hand and then was whisked to the operating room, where he wasn't allowed. There was a blur of green-clad nurses and doctors: the anesthesiologist, two obstetricians, and the pediatrician. I was given epidural anesthesia, so I was awake but groggy throughout. It all happened surprisingly quickly. Within a few minutes, I felt violent tugging in my abdomen, then a hard push just below the ribs. Then the lusty scream of a newborn baby split the air.

"Es una nina!" someone said. The nurse stood beside me holding a tiny wrapped bundle, and I beamed at the most beautiful baby I'd ever seen. It was a moment like no other. She tipped the scales at just five pounds, and had a perfectly round little head — just about the size of a large orange. (The cap I had crocheted fit.)

Hours later, when I could finally hold her for the first time, I knew I didn't have to worry anymore about what kind of mother I would be. Cradling her soft body against me and gazing into her serene face, her purplish veins visible through the translucent skin of her eyelids, I felt a fierce, protective love I'd never felt before. For the first time I could understand how a lioness or mother bear could kill or be killed to protect her young.

We named her Jane, after my mother. She was so tiny and needed feedings so often that for the first few weeks after we got home, we kept her beside our bed in a Moses basket. Before putting her down to sleep, I'd carry her in my arms and sing lullabies. The feel of her head heavy on my shoulder filled me with tenderness and awe that I'd been entrusted with the care of this fragile, helpless little being. I vowed to be the best mother I could be.

Jane grew rapidly and was—to me, anyway— infinitely precious and beautiful. As she grew, she was a happy and friendly toddler. She'd hold out her chubby arms to anyone, friend or stranger, human or animal. I started reading aloud to her when she was six months old, and her little green eyes would stare at the colorful pictures on the pages. At the same time I was careful not to spoil her or be overprotective. This child would grow up unafraid and independent. I devoured books and articles on raising children. I wanted to do everything right.

When Jane was five months old, I had gone on a long overdue visit home and spent three blissful months with my parents in Austin. When I'd gotten off the plane in the Dallas-Fort Worth airport, laden with baby and luggage, and heard that familiar Texas twang when the airport hostess asked, "Honey, could you use some help?" I almost fell into her arms and wept for joy.

On the ride home with my stepmother Nita and Daddy, I marveled at the tidy streets and the green well-manicured lawns of Texas. In my absence, the supermarkets had gone high-tech: now there were price scanners, some with human voices, and aisles and aisles of new products. A whole lexicon of catchwords had sprung up: what was a yuppie, a Pac-man? There was a bewildering alphabet of abbreviations I didn't know: what was a VCR,? a PC,? MTV? How did a microwave oven work? And what in heck was a Cabbage Patch doll? I was in culture shock for days, fascinated and a little overwhelmed by all the changes that had taken place in just three years.

I spent lazy days pulling weeds in the yard, with Jane in her ruffled sun rompers sitting on a blanket beside me. I spent lazy afternoons napping under the hum of the air conditioner. We arrived in August and stayed through Daddy's birthday on October 31. Federico joined us for the last two weeks of our stay. He had sold our Ford in La Paz for three times what we'd paid for it. We went on a shopping spree, buying clothes, a TV, a VCR, and a year's supply of everything from toothpaste to pantyhose. We had a long list of requests from friends and family in Bolivia. Our visit ended all too soon and in early November we were landing again in La Paz.

When she was a year old, I got pregnant again, and nine months later she had a baby brother, Michael. From the beginning there seemed to be a special closeness between them. In the hospital Jane gently laid her head against Michael's and grinned happily. I was alert to the possibility of sibling jealousy, but I never saw any signs of it. Michael was tiny at birth, too, but within six weeks he was robust and apple-cheeked. When they were old enough, we started going on daily walks, Michael in a stroller and Jane toddling alongside. Our favorite destination was the foot of a nearby hill where a pool of water was usually teeming with tadpoles. Over the weeks we watched the tadpoles develop into frogs. I delighted in the children's sense of wonder at all the new things they were discovering, and that wonder was reawakened in me, too.

Federico adored Jane and Michael. When he was home he would toss them into the air and cuddle them. But most of the time, they were already asleep by the time he got home from work at eight or nine. He didn't see much of me, either. He was content with his work, and I was occupied with raising two small children. It would've been a Herculean task without maids to help. Since we didn't have disposable diapers, one of the maids washed diapers and plastic pants every day, along with all the other clothes that a baby goes through every day. When both Jane and Michael were still in diapers things could get pretty hectic. Since I didn't have household chores to do, I could devote myself completely to taking care of the children.

Eventually, since I wasn't working, I got involved in other activities. Before Michael was born, I'd take Jane with me to the La Paz Community Church, where I'd play the piano in the

53

big empty sanctuary while Jane crawled around on the floor. Sometimes I served as the substitute pianist in church, and a couple of times a week I'd help out in the church office answering the phone and typing the weekly bulletin. The ladies' auxiliary ran a thrift shop and once a week we'd sort and price used clothes.

But my favorite activity was the monthly book club. With books ordered from the *New York Times Review of Books,* the La Paz Book Club provided a lending library for English speakers in La Paz. The meetings provided an opportunity for American, British and other English-speaking women to get together, eat home-baked goodies, and visit. We often sponsored programs with speakers, after which we'd hear club members review the latest books. I became a regular book reviewer and then volunteered to be on the selection committee. When I wasn't taking care of the kids, I was sitting on my bed with a book in one hand and a cup of *café con leche* in the other. It was a pretty cushy life, all told, and I enjoyed it. But after a while it didn't seem quite real. It got so that the lives of the characters in the books seemed more real than my own. My life revolved around my children, my books, and the all-too-rare letter from home.

When Michael was eight months old, I was offered a job with Food Aid International, a relief and development organization with an office in

La Paz. I wasn't ready to go back to work—I thought the children were still too young. But Federico and my in-laws talked me into taking the job. After all, it paid the unheard-of salary of $500 U.S. per month. I'd be crazy, they said, to turn it down. So I took it.

I became the coordinator for a child sponsorship program called Caring for Children. Through funds from sponsors in the U.S., Caring for Children supplied needy children with school supplies, shoes, and medical care. Sometimes it sponsored development projects to benefit an entire community. It was my job to plan and coordinate the program. It was the most challenging, interesting, rewarding, and frustrating job I'd ever had.

But Federico and I were beginning to grow further and further apart. He had his Bolivian friends; mine were American. When we talked, it was either about his work (he talked, I listened), or about the kids (I talked, he listened). I craved affection and warmth and attention, but he was too deeply involved with his other interests to notice. One afternoon I got an anonymous phone call from someone who claimed that Federico was having an affair with the pretty daughter of his boss. When I asked him about it, Federico brushed it off, saying that it must have been one of the union members at the factory trying to make trouble for him. I chose to believe him.

By then we'd been in Bolivia for more than five

years. Most of the American-Bolivian couples we knew when we'd first come to Bolivia had either split up or moved back to the United States. That we'd managed to stay together was no small feat in those times. But I felt increasingly isolated. I didn't remind Federico anymore that the two-year deadline for staying in Bolivia had long since passed. I knew that the more I complained, the more stubborn he would be. I decided to bide my time. One day he'd see for himself how bad things were and what a dead end it was, not only for me but for him, too. The turning point came when Federico was taken hostage at the factory by union members. Amid much media coverage he was released unharmed two days later. It was that episode that prompted him to decide that it was time to go back to the United States.

It took a year of untangling red tape for Federico to renew his resident's card. Finally all his documents were in order. We had a huge house sale and sold everything that wouldn't fit into our suitcases. Finally, we arrived in Austin. It was June 1985. My father set us up in a mobile home, rent-free, and Federico set about looking for work.

Things weren't as easy as we'd expected. The thrill of being home again quickly wore off as the hard realities of starting over set in.

By August our savings had dwindled alarmingly, and I was forced to take work as a legal secretary to support us. Seven months later, in January, Federico was finally offered a job with a large men's clothing manufacturer. We had to relocate to its plant in the Rio Grande Valley of Texas. Then, after Federico completed several months' training there as a production manager, we would have to move again, this time to the company's plant in the Dominican Republic.

I had misgivings about going right back to live in a third-world country just when I was finally home again, but I tried to make the best of it. The Dominican Republic was on a beautiful Caribbean island. It wasn't all that far from home. And it was a good career opportunity for Federico. For once he'd be earning a decent salary—in U.S. dollars this time, instead of in shrinking Bolivian pesos.

So in January 1986 we moved to McAllen, a small city on the Mexican border. Federico was soon absorbed completely in his new job and I stayed home and took care of Jane and Michael, now three and four. Since I wasn't working, I had plenty of time to think. Up until then I'd been so busy struggling to work and raise children and deal with the everyday problems of simple survival that I'd put off facing up to the problems in our marriage. I'd thought that after the stresses of living in Bolivia were behind us, our marital problems would magically disappear. Instead it brought them into sharper focus. I took a close look at our marriage and saw how hollow it was. Federico and I were barely friends and only infrequent lovers. Our single common bond, and the only topic we could discuss without arguing, was the children.

For years I'd been deeply frustrated with our relationship. Then I'd felt guilty for not being more content. After all, Federico didn't drink, beat me up, or chase women, at least, not that I knew of. He wasn't a bad person. So we had communication problems. So we didn't have much in common. So he was critical and took me for granted. Wasn't that true of many marriages? But it seemed that no matter how hard I tried to make things better, it was never enough.

I'd been the one to adapt to his country, his family, his customs and language. I'd put my own needs and interests on a shelf for eight years. And now if we went to the Dominican Republic I'd have to do it all over again. Was this the way it was going to be for the rest of my life? It seemed like a prison sentence. Yet, I argued with myself, marriage was a commitment. I'd promised eight years ago to stay with him, for better or worse. So I'd lost the toss and it was for worse . . . that was no excuse to bail out. I became adept at pushing my doubts to the edge of consciousness as soon as they surfaced, and went on being the dutiful wife.

One day in the summer of 1986 I read that the

book editor of the local McAllen newspaper wanted readers to send in book reviews. I wrote one and sent it in. Susan Espinoza, the editor, called me about my review. Beginning with that first telephone conversation we became friends.

Susan was a lanky redhead, from New England, who had graduated from Yale and spent summers at her parents place on an island in Maine. How she ended up married to a Mexican American and living in the sweltering Rio Grande Valley I never fully understood. But she never complained. Irrepressible, funny, outspoken, she didn't mince words, and I respected her.

She encouraged my writing, and when she went on vacation for three weeks, she asked me to take her place as book editor. The newspaper office — even in McAllen — was an exciting place, full of interesting characters. I'd always had a yen to be a reporter, and here I was rubbing elbows with them. Around this time I started taking ballet class again, too. It was exciting to be doing the things I loved again.

But Federico wasn't happy about it, and I wasn't sure why — maybe because it meant that on some days his supper wasn't on the table at six o'clock. He seemed to resent anything that took me away from him and the children, although when I was there he didn't pay much attention to me.

Now the date for moving to the Dominican Republic was fast approaching. I felt backed against a wall. Everything in me rebelled against going. Up until then I'd proven myself to be a master of procrastination. Now the time had come to make a decision. Would I be the supportive, adapting wife and once again put aside what was important to me? Or would I be selfish and go after what *I* wanted? There was a "right" choice, which filled me with despair, and a "wrong" choice, which filled me with hope and joy. Finally, I decided. I resolved to tell Federico that I'd made up my mind to stay behind with the kids while he went to the Dominican Republic.

To my surprise, it was Federico who saved me the trouble by announcing that we needed to have a talk. That evening, as soon as the kids were in bed, he faced me on the sofa and said, "I think I should go to the Dominican Republic by myself and you should stay here with the kids." Relief flooded through me. "We haven't been getting along for a long time, and I think we need to be apart and think things through. Besides, it would be better for Jane to finish her first semester in kindergarten here."

He went on, explaining how it would take all his concentration to learn his new job there, that his career was riding on it, and that he didn't need the hassles with me to distract him. By then we were fighting nearly every day.

When he finally finished, I told him I agreed.

If he was surprised at my answer, he didn't show it. We calmly discussed what he would take with him and what I would keep, and how much money he would send us each month. Then we agreed that at Christmas we'd discuss what to do next, whether to part ways or reunite in the Dominican Republic. We both admitted that we were tired of the fighting and needed peace and quiet to think things through. It was all neatly and civilly decided.

But we didn't count on opposition from his company. It was against its policy to relocate an employee without his family. They gave him an ultimatum—he could either go to the D.R. with his wife and children or be fired. Rather than cause him to lose his job, I agreed to go with him. We'd stay long enough for him to establish his position there, and then separate as planned. It was a stunning blow when the company fired him anyway. Around that time they were laying off a lot of managers, and since Federico was relatively new and giving them some cause for unease he was expendable.

After that Federico changed his mind about the separation. He didn't want to go through with it after all. He hadn't meant what he'd said earlier; he'd only been angry at me. For the first time in our relationship, he was the one doing the apologizing. He blamed himself for spending years too preoccupied with his job to pay attention to me, for being emotionally remote, and for various other problems.

A few years earlier, it might have been a good starting point. But now it was too late. All the procrastination and indecision was behind me. My mind was made up. I had to get away from him to think things through.

For the time being, though, we would have to call an uneasy truce. I couldn't very well kick Federico out in the street without a job. We were back to square one. I found another job as a legal secretary, the easiest job for me to get on short notice, and Federico was job hunting again. In addition to working as a secretary, I taught English to Mexican immigrants at a local elementary school in the evenings. In my "spare" time, late into the night, I typed Federico's applications and résumés.

The atmosphere at home was tense. Federico was still trying to make amends, to bridge the gap between us. But I knew that if I weakened and gave in, in time everything would go back to the way it had been before. I surrounded myself with an invisible shield, and nothing Federico said or did could penetrate it.

Until now. My thoughts swirled back to the present. I picked up the photographs of Federico and the children I'd taken out of the albums and slipped them into an envelope. Then I closed the albums and put them away.

That night the silence seemed to echo off the walls.

Chapter Five

Wednesday, November 18, 1987

The next day was spent in another tangle of red tape. At the FBI office we met with an agent who wore blue jeans and a beard, not at all my idea of what an FBI agent would look like. But I figured that since he was based in the Rio Grande Valley, he was probably doing drug undercover work. He took down the information that Mr. Rosenthal and I gave him and examined the photographs that I brought of the children and Federico. He explained that all he could do was to petition the U.S. Attorney's Office to issue a UFAP (a warrant alleging unlawful flight to avoid prosecution). Under a UFAP, Federico could be detained anywhere in the United States and brought back to Texas for prosecution. And what if he wasn't anywhere in the United States? I asked. The agent shook his head; once a fugitive got beyond the borders of the United States, even the FBI couldn't touch him.

In the meantime my father, also a lawyer, got a copy of the extradition treaty between the U.S. and Bolivia and sent me one. Parental kidnapping wasn't an offense under which a person could be extradited from Bolivia.

The next step was to call the State Department in Washington. I was directed to a businesslike young man in the Office of Consular Affairs. He told me there was nothing that the United States government could do to get my children back.

"They're under the jurisdiction of Bolivia now," he said matter-of-factly. "And especially since they were born there, they're considered to be Bolivian citizens. Bolivia will do everything in its power to keep them there."

"But they're *American* citizens too!" I protested. When they were only six weeks old I'd registered them at the U.S. Consulate and gotten them U.S. passports.

He went on in a neutral voice, "Of course, you could engage the services of a Bolivian lawyer and try to get legal custody of them through the Bolivian courts."

I knew how entrenched the corruption was in the Bolivian government and dismissed that option without a second thought.

"Isn't there anything else I can do? Can't my own country do anything to help me?"

"The only thing we have the authority to do is to send someone from the American Consulate to do a welfare and whereabouts check. They can try to find out where the children are and how they are being cared for." I asked him to arrange for the visit and gave him my mother-in-law's address. That was the most likely place for Federico to have gone. If only I knew for certain.

That week there were more trips to the courthouse and to the sheriff's office. A warrant for Federico's arrest was issued, and photographs of Federico and the children were wired to all international airports.

"By the way," Lisa Murillo, the investigator at the sheriff's office, said, "We ran a routine check on Mr. Bascope. Did you know he was arrested for shoplifting from a major department store in Austin in 1978?"

That had been a few months before we were married. "No, I didn't." I wondered again if I had ever really known him.

Several days later, with some inside help from a travel agent, we finally received a passenger list for a flight from Miami to La Paz dated November 14, 1987. I stared at the list in my hands, the first piece of concrete information we'd managed to get since their disappearance. There were their names in black and white—Freddy, Jane, and Michael Bascope—departed Miami Saturday, November 14, 1987—arrived La Paz, Bolivia, Sunday, November 15, 1987. Even before I had thought they were gone, they were irretrievably out of reach.

The phone was ringing. Twice, three times, six times. Silence again. A tiny sliver of light came through a gap in the curtains and pierced the darkness in the room. What day was it? Oh, yes, Monday . . . I should get up and go to work. But I couldn't get up. I should at least call in sick. I couldn't force myself to reach over and pick up the phone by my bed.

Gradually I became aware that my pillow was soggy. A steady stream of tears was sliding down the sides of my face. Had I been crying in my sleep? How strange. I dispassionately wondered about it for a moment. The tears kept coming, like a faucet left running in an empty house. My stomach growled, but the thought of food made me feel sick. I squeezed my eyes shut and tried to sleep again, to blot out awareness.

The phone rang again. I finally answered it.

"Hey, Cass, what's going on?" It was Mr. Rosenthal sounding like his usual cheerful self. "Aren't you coming to work today?"

"I don't think so."

"Why not?"

"Because. I just . . . can't." I couldn't gather

my thoughts sufficiently to give him a better answer.

"Are you still in bed?"

"Yes."

"Well, you can't just lie around all day. That's not going to do you any good."

"I know. I just need a little time."

More cheerfulness. "Hey, kid, we got a lot done in just one week's time." He ticked off our accomplishments: court orders, warrants, cables to all ports of exit from the United States, getting the process started for the FBI to issue a UFAP, getting hold of the airline records.

"I appreciate what you've done," I said. "None of it would have happened without you."

It was true. He had dropped everything to help me in that first week after Jane and Michael had disappeared. In the meantime, the law firm had gone forward without him at the helm. He was important. His time was valuable. I'd meant it when I'd said I appreciated all he'd done. What I didn't say was that the blizzard of court orders and writs and warrants—all the frantic activity of the week before—had given us only the illusion of accomplishing something toward getting my children back. In reality, even the long arm of Texas law could not stretch as far as Bolivia. Jane and Michael might as well be on the moon.

Mr. Rosenthal persisted. "When do you think

you'll be coming in. Tomorrow? You've got work to do, you know."

"I don't know." Couldn't think . . . didn't want to think.

"Do you need anything?"

"No, I'm OK."

"Have you eaten anything?" He'd learned that the first thing to shut down when I was upset was my appetite.

"Yes," I lied. If he knew the truth, he'd probably send Kathy over with food. She'd already done that once. I didn't want anybody to be bothered. I just wanted to be left alone.

"Well, call if you need anything. Okay?"

"I will. And—thank you. I appreciate your checking on me." "Appreciate" was such a pallid word for all he'd done. I tried again. "I . . . I owe you so much."

"Cass, you don't owe me anything."

But the truth was that I was immensely indebted to him. Not only the hours he'd spent with me, worth thousands of dollars in attorney's fees, but also court costs and deposition costs that he'd paid out of his own pocket because I didn't have the money to pay for them. Even more important were the intangibles: his advice, consolation, reassurance—basic hand-holding, I guess you'd call it. Being a friend to me in a town where I didn't have many friends. Being my family when I was hundreds of miles from my nearest relative. He'd had no idea what he was taking on when he agreed to take my case.

I remembered the first time I'd sat in his office, feeling a bit intimidated. He often had that effect on people. Not that he wasn't friendly. He'd stride through the office and boom greetings right and left, leaving a trail of cigar smoke in his wake. But he was also known for not suffering fools gladly.

So it was with some trepidation that I'd faced him that first day after he'd agreed to take my case. It was embarrassing to trot out the story of my failed marriage again; I'd already gone through it with my first lawyer. And here I would have to do it all over again, and what was worse, with someone I worked with and saw every day.

Mr. Rosenthal sat back in his chair, listening and asking an occasional question. I told him Federico had filed for divorce back in February. He'd given me custody of the children in his divorce petition. Then, three months later, he'd suddenly decided he wanted custody, and he'd asked the court for a jury trial to decide the issue.

"Hmm," Mr. Rosenthal had mused. "I don't know much about family law, but it's unusual in a custody case to ask for a jury trial. Normally the judge would be the one to decide that."

"That's one of the things that worries me," I said. "Down here you know that juries are 90 percent Hispanic. I'm afraid they'll side with him because he's Hispanic, too."

Mr. Rosenthal leaned forward and knocked the ashes off the end of his cigar. The pungent fragrance of it filled the room.

"That shouldn't make any difference. In fact, a predominantly Latin American jury would base its judgments on traditional values—it would be more likely to favor the mother keeping her children, unless she's done something they consider pretty bad." He lifted his eyes to mine. "Have you done anything that falls into that category?"

I met his gaze, but my hands were twisting in my lap. This was what I'd been dreading.

"He . . . he accused me of adultery, of seeing another man."

Mr. Rosenthal's face didn't change expression. "Were you?"

"Well, after he moved out, I started going out with somebody, yes. I thought it was okay—I know he was dating, too."

"Yes, but technically you were still married."

"I guess it wasn't the smartest thing to do," I admitted.

"No, not under the circumstances."

"Actually, Federico knew I was seeing somebody weeks before he ever filed for custody of the kids. So the fact that I was seeing somebody wasn't the issue."

"How did he find out?"

"He asked me and I told him."

Mr. Rosenthal groaned. Count on a lawyer to expect you to consider the consequences of your every move on a possible lawsuit.

"If he already knew, what made him file for custody all of a sudden, weeks after the fact?"

"Somebody told him that Brian was a drug dealer. But he's not, of course," I added quickly.

"At least not that you know of," Mr. Rosenthal corrected. He took another puff of his cigar. I wondered what he must be thinking of me. It all sounded so tawdry.

I shook my head. "I *know* he's not. Anyway, right after Federico filed for custody of the kids, his lawyer offered to make me a deal: if I agreed never to see Brian again, he'd give up his custody suit. I didn't want to risk losing my kids, so I agreed. But my former lawyer advised me not to. He said Federico had no right to tell me who I could and couldn't see."

"Have you quit seeing this guy?"

"Yes. My lawyer advised me not to see Brian anymore, anyway, so as not to give Federico any more ammunition." "Ammunition" was a good word to describe it—the whole thing had turned into a battle, with the kids caught in the crossfire. Besides, breaking it off with Brian hadn't done any good. Federico had remained convinced I was still seeing him.

It was much later, after the custody war had gotten complicated and ugly and after we knew each other better, that Mr. Rosenthal asked me in exasperation why I'd ever gotten involved with Brian in the first place. Why couldn't I have waited a few months?

Why, indeed?

It was an age-old story, as common as mud. Women got into affairs with a man they could talk to, a man who would listen. It happened all the time. But I thought I was the last person on earth such a thing could happen to, and Brian the last person on earth it could happen with. I'd met him in the public library. He was putting himself through college by working there as a reference librarian. When I was doing research for book reviews, he'd help me find information. In spite of the fact that he was ten years younger than I was, we became friends.

He was polite and a little shy at first. He was not conventionally handsome, yet when he smiled his eyes crinkled and he looked like a mischievous boy. I started looking forward to my trips to the library. As soon as he saw me, Brian would drop whatever he was doing and come to see what I needed, grinning from ear to ear. As time passed I began to notice that I was attached to him as well. I told myself I was imagining things: what could Brian possibly see in me, an older woman with two kids in tow, when he could have his pick of younger girls?

Brian made me feel beautiful, fascinating, and

desirable, and around him I became so. He thought I was perfect, and he let me know it. He'd wonder aloud what he'd done to deserve me, and I wondered the same thing. We seemed to understand each other without speaking, yet we could talk about anything. His impertinent sense of humor made me laugh, yet he had a quiet integrity and wisdom beyond his years. We seemed to bring out the best in each other, nurturing the good and ignoring the bad. Brian told me once that he wouldn't want to change anything about me, even my faults, because they were a part of me too. And he was a wonderful lover—tender, intense, playful. I couldn't have prevented myself from falling in love if I'd tried. And I didn't try. For once in my life I didn't weigh the pros and cons and go into paroxysms of indecision. I let myself tumble into it without a thought for tomorrow. I gave to him without considering what I'd get in return, and paradoxically I got everything.

Yet I knew that it wasn't something that would last forever. I had already seen how love's first bloom always faded into something altogether different, and I couldn't stand the thought of that happening to us. We never asked questions. We didn't make any rules and we took nothing for granted. I never lived so nearly in the moment as I did then, suspended in time and space.

I didn't try to explain all this to Mr. Rosenthal.

I was sure that he saw it simply as an affair. The word was so bald and ugly. *It wasn't like that at all,* I wanted to tell him. But Mr. Rosenthal brought me back from my reverie with more down-to-earth questions and we moved on to other topics of discussion.

During that second week after the children disappeared, I spent days in bed and managed to remain barely conscious most of the time. Sleep was a great escape, except for the dreams. I'd wake up with a vague feeling of foreboding but with no memory of what I'd been dreaming. Except for one vivid nightmare in which I was desperately searching the narrow gray streets of La Paz. In one of those dreams I finally found Jane and Michael in a schoolyard, and they stared at me without recognition. Afterward, I woke up in a cold sweat.

Mr. Rosenthal called once or twice a day to check on me. One morning, toward the end of the week, our conversation started out as usual.

"Cass, can I expect to see you in the office today?"

"No. Not today." There was silence for a moment.

"Cass, you gotta snap out of it. Don't let him win. He's got your kids—don't let him get you too."

Why not? I thought. Who cares about winning now? Sometimes the pain was so unbearable that I almost wished I wouldn't wake up and have to face it again. But I didn't voice that thought. Instead I said, "I just need a little more time."

"Time for what?" He was starting to sound exasperated.

"I guess to grieve."

"They're not dead, for Christ's sake!"

"It's almost as if they are. They're gone. I may never see them again."

"Cass, you'll see them again. I promise you that. It might be six months from now, or a year, or ten years from now. But you'll see them again."

Even six months seemed an eternity, an unendurable absence. At their age, they changed so fast. In six months' time they would be different people altogether. A picture of Michael as I'd last seen him flashed across my mind. He was hugging my knees, his upturned face grinning, freckles sprinkled across his nose. How he hated those freckles! I'd get him dressed and combed for church, and tell him, "Michael, you sure look handsome." He'd stand scowling in front of the mirror, and grumble, "Except for my freckles."

And Jane, my "princess and the pea," so sensitive that any little bump or scratch would make her toss and turn all night. How many times had I examined a patch of skin for an invisible bug bite? What must be going through her impressionable mind now?

I'd read about what happens when children are kidnapped. In six months' time, like hostages, they would form a strong bond with Federico. They would have no choice but to transfer all their love and trust to the person upon whom they were dependent. And who knew what Federico was telling them to hurry the process along—to chip away at their memories of me.

And then the next most painful thought sprang up: in time they would forget me. They were so young. But I would not forget. I confided these thoughts to Mr. Rosenthal.

"How can they forget you?" he asked gently. "You're too much a part of them. When I saw Michael that day in the office, I saw your sense of humor in him. The sparkle in Jane's eyes—that comes from you. They'll always have you with them."

He went on, "Cass, you might *not* see them for a long time. Look, I don't know what you believe. But I believe that people eventually get what they deserve. He won't get away with this. Someday it'll all come back to him."

Suddenly I felt unutterably weary. I didn't want revenge. Hadn't there already been enough suffering?

"Cass, you can't just lie down and die. You've got to pick yourself up and get on with things."

"I will. But right now I just can't. I know it's hard for you to understand."

Mr. Rosenthal was always so full of spark and energy, and he'd never faced real personal tragedy before. He was successful, happily married, with three bright and accomplished children. He'd never lost a loved one—even his parents were still alive.

"Maybe I can't. But I'll try," he said.

Trying to marshall my thoughts, I spoke slowly. "Imagine the very worst thing that could happen to you—whatever that is—something so terrible that you fear and dread it above anything else. Something so bad that you can't stand to think about it or hear about it or be reminded it could happen. Then—imagine it does."

There was silence for a few moments. He simply stayed on the line as I wept. Maybe in the silence he was crying too. I was very touched by this man's solicitude and persistence. Like the biblical story of Job, after all the haranguing and advising from Job's friends, they finally fell silent and simply sat with Job through his sufferings. There was nothing more comforting they could have done. In the same way, Mr. Rosenthal was there with me as I passed through my own dark valley.

The Plan

Chapter Six

It was the third week after Jane and Michael disappeared that I was ready to take action again. I started back to work — if you could call it work. As a paralegal I was supposed to bill a certain number of hours a day to the cases I worked on. Instead my timesheet lay practically untouched as I made phone calls and wrote letters and plotted strategy about the only thing I could concentrate on: how to get Jane and Michael back.

Mr. Rosenthal continued to be my lifeline. Once a day we'd sit in his office and discuss whatever I wanted to talk about. He tried to help take my mind off things and make me laugh — and, amazingly, he succeeded. On the other hand, many of my co-workers seemed to be avoiding me. They weren't being unkind. I think they were simply reacting as people often do in the face of someone else's misfortune, and they just didn't know what to say or do. Others were free with their advice. One of the lawyers at the firm had a black belt in karate; he offered to hunt down Federico and give him a fatal chop to the neck. That kind of talk made me uneasy. Although by now I hated Federico for what he'd done—it was easy to imagine gleefully emptying a revolver into him—I didn't really wish him harm. All I wanted was to get my children back. And I wanted to do it in a way that would spare them any further trauma.

I'd read an article about a woman who'd hired mercenaries to rekidnap her daughter from South Africa. She got her daughter back all right—after a hair-raising tug-of-war between the mercenary and the father, with the child screaming in the middle. I didn't want Jane and Michael to go through anything like that. Besides, through discreet inquiries Mr. Rosenthal had already found out that such an undertaking required money—*lots* of it. I didn't have that kind of money. And I knew I couldn't do it by myself. Bolivia was a military dictatorship with heavily guarded borders and police checkpoints everywhere. Federico had had it easy. All he had to do was put the kids on a plane and fly away. I knew it would be much more complicated to get them out of Bolivia.

Besides, it was my nature to do things by the book, to play by the rules. I decided to pursue a different course of action, one that was perhaps less dramatic but one that I thought would produce results.

I started a letter-writing campaign to Federico's relatives. I spent hours writing laboriously worded letters in Spanish to them all: his sister Ana Maria, his brothers Edgar and Rene, my sister-in-law Lily, and Nila. Surely they would listen to me. From the beginning Mr. Rosenthal dismissed my project as a waste of time and postage. In the end he was, of course, absolutely right. Not one of them answered.

At the same time I was writing them letters, I began trying to telephone them directly. My friend Susan volunteered her pleasantly cluttered house to place the phone call, and to serve as emotional support. She was also my language backup, in case in the heat of the moment I forgot how to speak intelligible Spanish, which she spoke better than I did. This was a humbling fact, considering she'd spent only two years in Spain compared with my six-and-a-half years in Bolivia.

Trying to place a long-distance call to Bolivia was always a hit-or-miss proposition. Sometimes you could try for days and never get through, and sometimes you could get through on the first attempt. This particular time, the line crackled and I faintly heard Nila's voice as she answered.

"This is Catherine," I began in Spanish. There was a short pause, then Nila unleashed a flood of angry words. Among other things she demanded to know why I had "done it." Done what? I wondered, and then realized she must be referring to something Freddy had told her. Ignoring that, I plunged ahead.

"Are Jane and Michael there with you? Is Federico living there with you?" I asked.

"No, they have not arrived yet. They are not here." *Yet* . . . that meant they must be on the way. She went on in a strident voice, telling me that the children were among family, that they were loved and well cared for and would lack for nothing.

"Except a mother," I said. "They won't have a mother. Did you know that Freddy took the children away from me without my knowing? Did he tell you he kidnapped them?" Nila was silent for a moment as she absorbed this. Maybe it was news to her.

"Freddy had no right to take Jane and Michael away. He's committed a serious crime in this country." My worries about not remembering the language disappeared, as I slipped into the idiom that used to come more easily to me than English. I struggled to maintain control of my quivering voice as I reminded her of how she used to praise me for being such a good mother. How could she think I had changed so much?

"No matter what Freddy has told you, I'm still a good mother. Freddy had no right to make the

84

children pay for our problems." Nila continued with vague accusations about how we never should have left Bolivia in the first place, but she didn't seem so sure of herself as she had a moment before. She sounded confused.

A new fear arose in my mind: what if he'd told Jane and Michael that I didn't want them? What if he'd told them I didn't love them anymore, as justification for taking them away?

"Please," I begged. "Tell the children that I love them."

She said that she would. Then there was a dial tone. She had hung up.

Shaking, I laid the receiver back in its cradle. Susan put her hand on my shoulder. "You did well. You said all the right things. You didn't even need me."

But what had I accomplished? Nothing, except to find out that — sooner or later — Jane and Michael would show up at Nila's house. Maybe she was lying and they were already there. If so, it meant Federico had no intention of letting me talk to them.

For a few more days I kept calling Nila to find out whether the children had arrived. She began hanging up as soon as she heard my voice.

I then turned to Federico's brother Edgar. He was devoted to his own two children, and so, I reasoned, he would understand my anguish.

Maybe he would reason with Federico's family on my behalf. During our first phone call he was as soothing and sympathetic as I'd hoped he'd be. He told me that Jane and Michael were with Federico in Tarija.

"Don't worry, Catherine, the children are fine. I'm sure they'll be back soon. I am sure that Freddy will let you talk to them as soon as they arrive in La Paz."

I called him every few days for an update, and he strung me along for two weeks with the same story. Mr. Rosenthal was skeptical but said little. I guess he didn't want to burst my bubble, figuring it would eventually collapse on its own.

Meanwhile, early in December, I also called an old American friend in La Paz, Russ Hall. When I was working at Food Aid International, Russ had been a volunteer there. I didn't know Russ as well as some of the other volunteers, even though we both worked in the La Paz office. He was unobtrusive and softspoken. He had wanted to go and live among the Bolivian peasants like the other volunteers, but because he was a CPA, FAI thought he'd be more useful in the central office. After his two years of service were up, he volunteered for two more years. When the director of FAI for Bolivia resigned, the directors in Geneva asked Russ to take his place. Now, after most of the other volunteers I'd known had gone back home, Russ was still in Bolivia.

He said he would help—he would talk to Edgar to try to find out what was really going on. When I called back a few days later, Russ had already been to see Edgar.

"He acted like he really wanted to help," Russ said. "But he told me the same thing he's been telling you—that Freddy and the kids are in Tarija and they'll be back any day."

"Is that all? Did he say anything else?"

"Well, yes . . ." Russ seemed reluctant to discuss it.

"What else?"

"Apparently Freddy told him some pretty bad things about you."

He didn't have to go into details. I knew what they were: I neglected the children. I left them alone at night and then came home drunk. I had a boyfriend who was a drug dealer, or else I had an eighteen-year-old boyfriend. Or he might have combined the two and said that I had an eighteen-year-old drug dealer boyfriend. Or maybe he'd told Edgar the continuous-stream-of-one-night-stands story. I was pretty sure that Federico had told Edgar some variation on one of these. Of course, none of it was true. But Federico was good at talking. I was sure he'd convinced his family of whatever he'd said. Maybe he'd even convinced himself.

Russ kept checking with Edgar every few days,

and Edgar kept telling him the same thing. But one day in mid December when I called Russ he had different news.

"Cassie, I saw Jane and Michael. They're in La Paz."

My throat squeezed shut. "Where?"

"They were walking down a street with Freddy, in Obrajes." Obrajes was a residential area of La Paz. We'd rented a house there during our last few years in Bolivia.

"How did they look?"

"They seemed to be fine. Jane and Michael were walking in front of Federico. They were holding hands.

I wept with relief. Finally my imagination had an image to hold onto, and surroundings to place them in. I was grateful that Jane and Michael were so close. They would stick together and be a comfort to each other.

"After I saw them I called Edgar, to see if he'd tell me the truth," Russ continued. "But he told me the same story about the children being in Tarija." So much for Edgar the mediator. "Apparently he's been lying all along."

There was still one brother left to approach: Manuel, the psychologist in West Berlin. Before Federico and I were married, he had visited us once in Austin. We'd given him a Texas-style tour and Manuel, despite his rudimentary knowledge of English, entered readily into the spirit of things. He did the Cotton-Eyed Joe at a country-western honky-tonk, ate enchiladas at a Mexican restaurant, and in nearby San Antonio, toured the Alamo and strolled the Riverwalk along the San Antonio River. Manuel was sensible and intelligent and *human*. Surely *he* would listen.

I wrote a long letter to him. After weeks without a reply, I decided he wasn't going to answer. Then one morning at 3 A.M., Manuel called.

"Catereen?"

"Yes," I said groggily.

"This is Manuel." Then he began speaking in Spanish. "I received your letter. I knew that Freddy and the children were in La Paz, but I did not know that he'd kidnapped them from you. That is not the correct way to do things." He promised to talk to Federico in April, when he and his wife would be traveling to La Paz.

April seemed a long way off. Still, if anyone could convince Federico of how damaging all this was to the children, it was Manuel. Yes, I thought, they would listen to Manuel. Logic and reason would prevail at last.

After appealing to Federico's family in every way I could think of, I threw myself on the mercy of the Catholic Church. I made an appointment to see Father Ivan, a Cuban priest at the Catholic Church Federico had attended in McAllen. If I could get the Church to intervene on my behalf, I thought, Federico's family would surely listen. After all, they were Catholic. Nila was especially devout — early each morning she walked several blocks to attend Mass. A priest's word would carry a lot of weight with her.

Father Ivan was a big man, tall and heavily built, with thinning gray hair and a no-nonsense manner. I explained the situation briefly and asked if he would help.

He spoke with a slight Cuban accent. "I didn't know Mr. Bascope very well. I was a little put off by him, actually. He made an appointment to see me, to talk about his divorce. The first thing he said was that he came to me, a priest, because he couldn't afford a *real* psychologist." Father Ivan shrugged. "Then he quit coming because I wouldn't do what he wanted me to."

"What was that?"

"He thought I should call you and persuade you to go back with him. I told him that I cannot do things that way. Then he quit coming."

Father Ivan said he would do what he could. The Vatican had a papal nuncio in La Paz. Father Ivan would get in touch with someone there, and that priest would in turn contact Federico.

"The only thing we can do is try to persuade him to meet with you somewhere and discuss a compromise." Father Ivan's brows drew together. "But I don't think that you should go to Bolivia for such a meeting. Ugly things could happen to you there."

I knew he was right, but such incidents were usually politically motivated. I couldn't imagine Federico carrying out anything so evil. But then again, during the past year he'd done many things I couldn't have imagined him doing.

After my conversation with Father Ivan, I was buoyed with hope once more. But as the weeks passed, this faded. Eventually, a priest in La Paz did call Nila, but instead of bowing obediently to the wisdom of the Church, she told the priest that it was her son's business and she didn't want to be involved in it. Apparently feeding and sheltering Federico and the children didn't count as involvement.

Time passed slowly. I couldn't get used to the stillness of the apartment. Where once there had been a constant stream of neighborhood children running in and out, now the doorbell fell silent. No toys were strewn across the living room, no fingerprints smudged the door. I didn't have to hurry each morning, waking the children up, getting them breakfast, getting them dressed for school. I didn't have to rush home to cook supper, run baths, pack lunches. Like all mothers of young children, I never seemed to have any time for myself, except in those precious hours after they were in bed at night.

Now I had all the time I could ever want. The only problem was I couldn't remember what it was I had been so eager to do. I never touched my ballet slippers again after the last "Ugly Duckling" performance. I quit writing book reviews. I didn't even read very much anymore.

At some point I shut the door to the children's room so I wouldn't have to look into it at every turn. Mr. Rosenthal urged me to pack up their toys and clothes. Kathy offered to come over and help me do it. But that would have been an admission of defeat, so I left their room as it was. Sometimes I'd go into it, walk around, and touch their things. I'd bury my face in their still unwashed sheets, where the scent of their bodies was becoming fainter and fainter.

For my birthday at the end of November, Mr. Rosenthal had had a lush ficus tree delivered to my apartment. Its branches were heavy with thousands of shiny green leaves. But almost at once, the leaves began to fall off. I knew that a certain amount of shedding was normal, but when it continued, I called the plant nursery for advice. They gave me careful instructions about watering and lighting and I followed them to the letter. Still, every day there was a new pile of dead leaves around the tree. Every few minutes throughout the day a rustling sound would signal the falling of another leaf.

The tree was dying. It began to take on an almost symbolic significance for me, as if some kind of dry rot had taken over my life and was blighting everything I did.

I was tortured by what Mr. Rosenthal called "the whuff-its." What if I hadn't been so caught up in "doing my own thing"? What if I'd called the children that Saturday instead of helping out at the theater? What if I'd monitored airline reservations, kept closer tabs on Jane and Michael, done a thousand other things that might have made a difference?

There was no comfort to be found in my faith, either. All of a sudden I found it very difficult to pray. Had I displeased God? Was He punishing me by taking away what was most precious to me?

Of course, none of it explained why the children should suffer. I was seven years old and my mother was thirty-six when she died. Now I was thirty-five and Jane was six. Was history repeating itself? Was there some kind of hidden logic in it all? My mind ran in circles. For the first time in my life, I felt completely helpless to change my situation. Every avenue I'd tried had come up a dead end. I began to develop a fatalistic attitude.

One day at lunch, I told Kathy how I felt. She had just told me that she'd prayed for me every day.

"What do you pray for?" I asked.

She looked surprised. "Well, for you to get your kids back, of course."

I wound a strand of spaghetti around my fork. One end of it kept slipping off.

"Maybe it's not supposed to happen. I'm afraid to pray for what I want anymore. I prayed that we wouldn't have to go through a jury trial, and I got what I wanted. But look how it happened. I'm afraid that if I pray for the kids to come back, it'll happen, but in some terrible way." A picture of little coffins being unloaded from a plane flashed across my mind. "Or maybe I'll get them back but it won't be good for them, living here. Maybe for some reason I'll never know, they're better off with Federico in Bolivia, and that's why the whole thing happened."

Kathy frowned and stabbed at her food.

I went on. "I know that I want them. But so does Federico. Why should God listen to my prayers and ignore his? So I just pray that His will be done and leave it at that."

"I admire your Christian attitude. If I were in your shoes, I wouldn't give a hoot what Federico wanted," Kathy said.

I laughed bitterly. "There's nothing Christian

about it."

In fact I had never felt so far away from God. He had abandoned me — or maybe, in shame, I had hidden myself from Him. Maybe I'd brought it all on myself and now I was stewing in the foul juices of my own contriving. I had deep feelings of guilt for my role in breaking up our marriage. Had I behaved selfishly? I'd have to answer "yes."

I'd gone over all these feelings both with my pastor and Mr. Rosenthal. They both made the same observation: it was probably inevitable. I had reached my limit and the dam had broken. I spent a lot of time brooding about the whys and wherefores of it all. Why was it that we women think we have to put up with things until we can stand them no longer? Don't we deserve to enjoy our lives, too, instead of sacrificing them on the altar of marriage and motherhood? But my first attempts at enjoying life seemed to have brought me nothing but trouble. And what about those good old-fashioned virtues like duty and loyalty and fidelity? Where did they fit in? It was all so confusing.

In the meantime, I settled into a routine again. I went to work and to church and occasionally visited Kathy or Susan. I started seeing Brian again, and his tenderness got me through many a lonely time. Even people I hardly knew were kinder. They'd tell me how well I was taking the loss of my children. They'd praise me for my courage and dignity. On the outside I seemed "together." On the inside there was a gaping emptiness that nothing could fill. I struggled against the seductiveness of people's sympathy. It would've been easy to slip into the role of the martyr and use that as an excuse for failing to get on with my life. I'd find myself sliding into the slough of despondency and then, disgusted, haul myself out again.

I ached for my children, yet it seemed all I could do was wait and hope.

As Christmas approached I felt almost desperate to see Jane and Michael, even if it meant going to Bolivia. Mr. Rosenthal discouraged the idea.

"What in the world would you accomplish by doing that?"

"They'd know I still care. I could take some Christmas presents for them, too. You know how important presents are to kids."

"What makes you think that guy would let you see them?" Mr. Rosenthal avoided granting Federico the dignity of calling him by name. "He won't even let you talk to them on the phone."

"How could he say no if I just showed up at their doorstep?"

Mr. Rosenthal shook his head, exasperated.

"For one thing, it's a bad idea to go by yourself. That bastard is capable of anything. For another, it would be terrible to see those kids and then have to turn around and leave them again."

I had already talked about this with Kathy and Susan. As mothers, they agreed with me: even if I couldn't get close to the kids, I could shout at them, do *something* to let them know I'd made the effort. Even that would be worth the trip. Both women also correctly anticipated Mr. Rosenthal's response.

"You'd spend all that money—airfare must be more than a thousand dollars—and for what?"

"To see their faces, to see for myself that they're all right, reasonably happy, well cared for. To let them know I haven't forgotten them."

Mr. Rosenthal leaned forward and spoke more gently. "Look, Cass, you've held up pretty well so far. But if you went all the way down there and only got to see them from a distance, you wouldn't be able to handle it. I wouldn't be able to handle it, if it were me."

So I didn't go. On Christmas Eve, I made one of my periodic attempts to call Nila. To my surprise, she talked to me this time. She was even civil. She explained that Freddy and the children were out, but that they'd be back by six o'clock. But when I called back at six, there was no answer.

A few days after Christmas, I got a report

from Paul Anderson at the State Department. Someone from the American consulate had finally visited the children. Paul told me that he had received a long cable from La Paz, saying that the children were indeed living with their father in Nila's high-rise condominium. They seemed to be healthy and well cared for. Had the consular representative made it clear to the children that he had come on my behalf? I asked. Yes, they'd told the children that their mother had requested the visit. Anderson added that according to the cable, Freddy had been pleasant and cooperative.

He must be feeling pretty confident, I thought. Well, at least he wasn't hiding out. And it was a relief to know the kids were all right. But I got the feeling Anderson wasn't telling me everything he knew. The cable was long, but he'd told me only a few things. Too many questions were left unanswered.

It wasn't long before I got another report, this one from Russ.

"Cassie, I just wanted to tell you that I delivered your Christmas package to Jane and Michael."

Finally! A first-hand report on how they really were! I squeezed the receiver against my ear to hear him better through the long-distance static. "Did you give them the presents?"

"They didn't open the box while I was there.

But I told Jane and Michael it was from you."

I had sent a box of presents in care of Russ, thinking that if I sent it to Federico, he might not give it to the children. I'd packed some of Jane's and Michael's old toys as well as new ones, and their favorite pajamas. Tucked throughout were little notes from me, saying that I loved them and missed them. There were also some Christmas cards that Michael's preschool class had drawn for him, and letters from both children's teachers in McAllen. In an attempt to soften up my in-laws, I packed tins of Christmas cookies for them, and—even though it galled me—threw in a box of Triscuits, Fedrico's favorite snack food.

Russ told me that Federico and Nila welcomed him in and even invited him to stay for lunch. From Nila he got an enormous midday meal, and from Federico he got a first-hand recital of my past sins, real and imaginary.

"How were Jane and Michael?" I asked.

"They were a little shy. I don't think they remembered me." Russ and the other volunteers had been at our house a few times when we lived in La Paz.

"What did they say when you told them the box was from me?"

"They didn't say much. They were pretty quiet."

"Did you tell them that I love them?" I had

asked Russ to be sure to remember that.

"Yes, I told them that two or three times."

"Did they seem to be okay? Pretty happy?"

"Yes."

I was relieved, but at the same time my heart ached—had they already forgotten me? Russ said that when he brought up the subject of me visiting the children, Federico and his mother were cordial but adamant: there would be no compromise—Jane and Michael would stay in Bolivia with their father, and the sooner they forgot about me, the better.

Chapter Seven

About a month had passed since I'd seen my children. My strategies to get through to Federico and his family through common sense and persuasion had come to nothing.

I called the State Department and talked again to Paul Anderson. He gave me some disheartening facts: there were hundreds of parents in my situation whose children had been kidnapped and taken to South America and other parts of the world. No extradition treaties for parental kidnapping existed between the United States and any Latin American country. My only chance of getting Jane and Michael back, Anderson said, was to go through the Bolivian court system.

He added parenthetically, "Unless you go down and kidnap them back. But of course the State Department couldn't have anything to do with that."

"How often does that happen—I mean, successfully?"

"We don't keep statistics on it," he answered shortly. "But I can tell you we don't recommend it. You could end up in a Bolivian prison, with even less hope than ever of seeing your children again. And the U.S. Government wouldn't be able to bail you out."

I was reminded of the maxim that if you find yourself in trouble in a foreign country, don't waste a phone call to the U.S. Embassy.

I asked him what he thought my chances were of recovering Jane and Michael legally.

"It depends on a lot of things. The laws and judicial system are similar to ours—on paper, anyway. In reality, it depends a lot on how influential your husband and his family are."

"Well, he knows a lot of people, the *right* people, I guess you'd say. He went to the best private school in the country. A lot of his old high school friends have held positions in the Bolivian Government. Maybe some are in it now." Never mind that in Bolivia, governmental appointees changed with bewildering rapidity. But I knew that the current President, Victor Paz Estenssoro, was from Federico's hometown, and that Federico had at least a passing acquaintance with him. In a country with such fierce regional loyalties as Bolivia, just being from the same town could carry a lot of weight. Great . . . he might have the President on his side, and maybe a couple of cabinet members to boot.

"If your husband doesn't have that much clout and can't prove that you were a bad mother, you have a chance."

"How often does that happen, that the American parent wins custody in a South American court?" I asked.

Paul replied blandly, "It could happen."

Not very encouraging. And there was another factor that he hadn't mentioned: bribery. This was what greased the ponderous wheels of the Bolivian bureaucracy—what motivated sullen, underpaid government employees to move things along. Even the most routine process, like getting a driver's license, required a dozen signatures and official seals, and often took several days. But with a little bribe money, even the driving test became optional. On the other hand, without bribes, the most trivial bureaucratic process could get bogged down indefinitely. But more than anything, working the system in Bolivia meant knowing the right people. And I, of course, was an outsider.

It didn't look good, but I didn't have any options left. I asked Anderson to send me a list of Bolivian attorneys. A few days later it arrived. I noticed the disclaimer on the first page with some misgivings: the State Department didn't recommend or guarantee any of the attorneys on the list. I picked the first lawyer on the list who practiced family law.

Dr. Victor Castillo answered the phone himself,

booming into the receiver in a rich baritone. For what seemed like the hundredth time, I explained the situation, this time in Spanish. Dr. Castillo (in Latin America, lawyers are addressed as "Doctor") seemed interested and knowledgeable. After I assured him that I had done nothing to deserve having my children taken away, he told me he was confident the Bolivian courts would do the right thing and give me my children back. He told me he would work closely with the U.S. Consulate on my case. First of all, he said, he would check with the courts to see if Federico had already filed any papers for divorce or custody. In the meantime, I should go ahead and get my divorce finalized and the decree should spell out in no uncertain terms that I was the parent with legal custody. Then I needed to get the decree "legalized"—translated and stamped by the nearest Bolivian Consulate. Finally I should send it to Dr. Castillo as soon as possible. As soon as he got the papers, he explained, he would simply argue before the Bolivian Supreme Court for the formal recognition of the U.S. custody decree, in a process known as a writ of exequator. Federico's petition would then be thrown out.

It seemed too easy.

"So you think there's a good chance that the Supreme Court will do that?" I asked.

"Oh, yes, you don't need to worry about that. I used to be a judge, and some of the Supreme

Court justices are my personal friends." Great! He *knew* people.

"Will I need to come down there to appear in court?"

"No, that won't be necessary. There won't be any hearing. The Supreme Court justices will simply sign the papers and that's it."

"How long will this whole process take?"

"In one month you should be able to come down and pick up your children."

My heart began to hammer. It was almost January now. That meant that as early as February I might see my children again!

Before concluding our conversation, Dr. Castillo asked for a $1000 retainer. Paul Anderson had said that I could expect to spend several thousand dollars in a lawsuit for custody. Under the circumstances $1,000 seemed quite reasonable. In fact, it was a bargain, if it resulted in the return of my children. I told Dr. Castillo that I'd send it as soon as possible.

Within a week my father got the money and I sent a cashier's check in that amount to La Paz. Filled with renewed hope and energy, I set about getting the necessary papers together.

Mr. Rosenthal was skeptical about the sort of justice meted out by Bolivian courts. But I was determined to play by the rules. I still thought that right would prevail. Besides, there would be so many advantages to recovering the children under Bolivian law. First of all, it would vindicate me. Federico, his family, and the world at large would see that his accusations were groundless and that I was a fit mother for Jane and Michael.

Second, he would never be able to kidnap them again, at least not with Bolivia as a safe haven.

Third, if Jane and Michael were peacefully handed over to me, it would save them from unnecessary trauma. I was even optimistic that some kind of enforceable agreement could be worked out so they could visit Federico on occasion. I would've been willing to let them spend their summers there, if I could be sure that — with the backing of the Bolivian Government — Federico would always return them to me. If at all possible, I wanted them still to have both a mother *and* a father.

But for now the first order of business was the divorce. I had been postponing it for months, mainly because as long as I was married to Federico I was considered a Bolivian citizen, and I thought it might be an advantage, especially if I went to Bolivia. Now it was more important for me to have permanent custody under United States law.

Mr. Rosenthal drew up the divorce decree carefully. He thought that if we were too emphatic in denying Federico his rights, the Bolivian courts might balk. The decree gave me exclusive parental rights to Jane and Michael, but didn't specifically deny Federico any. It also spelled out that Federico was still responsible for paying child support. Although we knew there wasn't much chance that he'd abide by that provision, it was a way to hold him liable under the law should he ever show up in the United States again.

It was a chilly day in January when Mr. Rosenthal and I went to the courthouse for the divorce proceedings. In Judge Villarreal's chambers, Mr. Rosenthal briefly explained the terms of the divorce decree and in the space of five minutes it was over. Judge Villarreal shook my hand and grimly wished me luck. Later that month, divorce papers and translations in hand, I flew to Houston to get them legalized at the Bolivian Consulate.

Finally everything was in order, and I sent the papers by International Federal Express to Dr. Castillo, along with a laboriously written letter in Spanish that explained the background of it all.

One day late in January when I dialed Nila's number, Federico answered. It took me by surprise. I hadn't spoken with him since the kidnapping. He was guarded, but civil. When I asked if I could speak to Jane or Michael, he still refused.

"When will I be able to? Are you *ever* going to let me talk to them?"

"Maybe after more time has passed." I could picture him as he spoke: green eyes cold, lips set in a rigid line. I knew that look well.

"Are you ever going to let me see them again?"

"I don't know. It is better for them if they just forget you."

Anger rose up in me. *No, don't let him get to you. You've got to play this right. Only through him can you reach Jane and Michael.*

I tried to appeal to his reason, if he had any left, to whatever bond might still exist between us. "Federico, if only we could've talked. All this could've been avoided if we could've just *talked* to each other. But you wouldn't listen. You had all these crazy ideas in your head—"

Wrong move.

"I knew the *truth!*" he shouted. "You fooled all your friends—you even had your lawyer fooled! But *I* knew what you were doing! Only *I* know the kind of person you really are!" Then he moved in for the kill: "Someday the kids will know too, and they'll hate you for it."

"What are you talking about? What was I doing?" It was turning into a replay of a dozen scenes from the previous summer.

"You and your drug dealer boyfriend," he sneered. "I know you were using drugs. Irene found some in your room."

Irene? She was the Mexican woman who had taken care of Jane and Michael while I was at work. She had worked for me for over a year. Why would she make up lies about me? It didn't make sense.

I struggled to remain calm. "Look, Federico. I don't know why Irene would make up something like that. But *think*. Use your head! You knew me for eleven years! Did I *ever*, in all that time, show the slightest interest in drugs?"

But he wasn't listening. He was off and running, shouting a stream of crude insults. I tried to break in a few more times, but it was no use. I hung up the phone and sat there, shaken. Why would Irene lie? Or if she didn't lie, what could she have possibly seen that she thought was evidence of drug use?

"Maybe Irene had a crush on Federico," Susan offered when I told her about it later. "Didn't he use to sit down and talk with her a lot before he moved out?"

It was true . . . Federico had always been much friendlier with Irene than I was. After years of trial and error in Bolivia, I'd learned that being businesslike was the best way to deal with maids. But maybe I'd made a mistake. Maybe I should have been more of a buddy instead of an employer.

Susan suggested, "Maybe Irene never said any such thing and he just made it up."

That was possible, too. He'd done it before. After he'd filed for custody, Federico had once called my pastor and told him an outlandish story about Michael knocking on a neighbor's door at 2 A.M., asking where his mommy was. According to

Federico, I'd gone out and left the children alone. In his scenario the neighbor summoned the police. No such thing had ever happened, except in Federico's imagination.

It was on February 2, 1988, a few weeks after my conversation with Federico, that I finally got to talk to the children themselves. Federico had answered the phone. To avoid getting into another senseless argument, I asked without preamble if I could talk to Jane and Michael. To my surprise, he said "Yes." I was struck numb with delight and apprehension. After all the weeks and months of fruitless phone calls, I would finally hear their voices again. I clutched the receiver, scarcely daring to breathe.

"Hello?" came a child's voice, sounding familiar and yet unfamiliar.

I struggled to control my voice. "Michael?"

A giggle, then, "No, this is Jane." She sounded so young, like such a baby.

"Jane, this is Mommy." There was so much to say, yet so little that I *could* say—Federico might be listening in. "How are you, honey?"

"Fine."

"I love you, Jane. I miss you."

"I miss you, too," she said dutifully.

"Did you get the things I sent you for Christmas?"

"Yes. I got the Barbie. And you know what else? Daddy got me a My Little Pony, the one I wanted." She went on, rattling off a list of what she'd gotten for Christmas. I drank in the sound of her voice. But there was something different about it. Then I knew: she spoke with an unmistakable Spanish accent. Her chatter wound down, and there was a short silence. "Do you want to talk to Michael now?"

"Yes. I love you. I miss you," I said again.

Then Michael's voice, even more high-pitched and babyish. "Hi, Mommy."

He was telling me something about swimming lessons. "But nee know what?" I'd forgotten he said "nee know what" for "you know what." "When we got in the water it was cold. I got scared and wanted to go home."

My heart quickened. "You wanted to come *home?* Here with me?"

He laughed. "No, Mommy. *Home.* With *abuelita.*"

I bit my lip. Of course. By now his grandmother's house was home. "How are the lessons now? Are you learning how to swim better?"

"Yes."

"Do you remember your swimming lessons here, when I took you to that big pool last summer?" Please remember the home you used to have, I silently pleaded.

But he was talking about his Christmas presents now. Then Federico was back on the phone.

"Thank you for letting me talk to them," I said,

my voice finally breaking.

"Take care," he said stiffly.

Reluctantly I laid the phone back into its cradle. Conflicting emotions wrestled within me. I could tell they were happy. They were fine, and I was immensely relieved for that. Yet how I had ached to hear them say, "Mommy, we miss you! Come get us. We want to go home!" I laid my head on the back of the chair as one sob after another tore out of me.

After that, for some reason, Federico let me talk to the children whenever I called. When I said I missed them and loved them, they dutifully parroted my words. As time passed, they began to seem a little more subdued with each call. What did that mean? That they weren't as happy as I thought? That they were forgetting me? Maybe they just didn't know what to say. Federico had already taken them from me physically. Now he was robbing me of their minds and hearts, too. I felt like I was standing on a shore shouting and waving as they sailed farther and farther out to sea. The calls left me drained and troubled for days afterward. I began to put off making them.

By this time, my confidence in Victor Castillo had begun to fade. In spite of all the doomsaying by Mr. Rosenthal and my family, I had clung to the belief that the law — even Bolivian law — would

112

be on my side. But as time went by, the bland assurances of Dr. Castillo started to sound hollow. What was supposed to take only a couple of months was taking much longer. In fact, he hadn't taken the first step yet, presenting my documents to the Bolivian Supreme Court. Dr. Castillo had plenty of plausible excuses for the delays: He had to get extra documents translated and legalized. The Supreme Court was not in session now. There was a general strike in the country, and offices were closed indefinitely. There was a transportation strike, and all flights to Sucre, the seat of the Supreme Court, were cancelled.

So much for following the rules.

Chapter Eight

It was a conversation we'd been having since early in December and were no closer to finishing on this particular Friday afternoon in February.

"Even if I had it, I wouldn't pay $100,000 for some sleazy mercenary to grab Jane and Michael. I wouldn't put them through that. It's worse than what Federico did."

"Well, *you* sure can't go down there," Mr. Rosenthal said, as he always did when I talked about going to Bolivia. What if I got thrown in jail and was left to rot forever in the bowels of some Bolivian prison? What if I got killed? That kind of thing happened.

Mr. Rosenthal was smart enough to know he couldn't persuade me with those arguments, so he tried to couch his counsel in terms I would listen to.

"It'd be stupid for you to go when there are professionals to do the job. What could you possibly do that they couldn't do better? Yes, the kids might be scared for a while. But they'd forget all about that once they saw you."

"Well, it's too early to think about all that. I'm going to wait and see what Dr. Castillo says next time I talk to him." I still had hopes for a legal solution. Mr. Rosenthal rolled his eyes and threw up his hands.

"You don't hear a thing I say," he griped, not for the first time. "I might as well be talking to that ashtray." He took a puff from his cigar, then said casually, "I know somebody who could do it."

"Who?" In spite of myself I was interested.

"A private investigator. Ex-FBI. He's done some work for the firm—locating missing witnesses, that sort of thing. Gayle knows him real well." Gayle was a rather flamboyant attorney at the firm. "All I can tell you is that this guy says he could do it."

"How do you know?"

"I've already talked to him. Whenever you decide it's time, I can arrange for you to meet him."

It was February of 1988. My weekly phone calls with Dr. Castillo made it clear that he hadn't done anything he'd promised to do. I still occasionally toyed with the idea of a resnatch, but only in theory. I didn't have the means to carry it out.

Then, the first miracle happened. The father of my stepsister Courtney—he had been an orthopedic surgeon in Houston—had died suddenly in January. Daddy had been handling the probating of his estate for Courtney. He called me one afternoon in February to tell me that as the only heir, Courtney had inherited a small fortune. One of the first things she wanted to do was use part of it to help me get Jane and Michael back.

When I broke the news to Mr. Rosenthal, he whistled softly. He voiced what was on both our minds. "Now you can hire somebody to go down and get the kids."

I didn't say anything.

"Well, Cass, what are you gonna do?" he persisted.

"I don't know." Now that the doors were opening, I was afraid to step through them. It had taken a lot of soul-searching to reach the relative equanimity I now felt, and the pain had finally subsided to a dull ache. After countless lectures from Mr. Rosenthal, I had finally reached the stage where I didn't wonder a hundred times a day where Jane and Michael were, what they were doing, what they were thinking.

Besides, I'd just about reached the conclusion for some reason I'd never understand, that they were better off in Bolivia with their father. Why else had every avenue been blocked? Why else had I run up against brick wall after brick wall?

"Cass, they're kids," Mr. Rosenthal would say to such doubts. "As long as they're reasonably well

116

cared for, they'll adapt wherever they are. But that doesn't mean they're better off there. They'd still be a hundred times better off with you. There's not a scrap of doubt in my mind about that."

Too bad I couldn't be as sure as he was. How nice it would be to be sure of something for a change. As it was, I'd learned to live with doubts, with not knowing or understanding. I'd heard somewhere that our job on earth was not to understand, but to live. That's what I'd been trying to do — to learn to accept the unacceptable, to live with the unlivable.

For a long time I'd felt a terrible gaping emptiness inside, and just when I thought there was hope, my guts would be ripped out all over again. I'd been peeled like an onion, layer after layer, until now I was exquisitely sensitive to the slightest touch. Before, I'd rarely cried. Now, anything could make me cry — a pretty passage of music, the sight of purple bougainvillea in bloom, a line of poetry. Everything was so precious to me now, maybe because I knew it could all disappear in an instant. Now I didn't count on anything; I didn't expect anything. I didn't waste my time trying to mold people or circumstances to the way I wanted them to be. I tried to enjoy what there was, here and now, because that was all I could count on.

Yet a door had opened. This might be my last and only chance. I couldn't turn my back on it. I took a deep breath.

"Okay, I'll talk to this guy. I want to see what he has in mind. But *if* I decide to hire him, it would be on one condition: that I'm the first one to lay hands on the kids."

Mr. Rosenthal ignored my last statement, but he looked pleased. A few days later he told me that the private investigator, whose name was Lloyd Barber, would be in town Friday. He could see me that evening after work.

At 5:05 P.M. on Friday, March 4, 1988, I waited nervously in the unaccustomed grandeur of Mr. Patton's office. Since he was out of town, Mr. Rosenthal had designated his office as the meeting place for Mr. Barber and me. Unlike the contemporary office of Mr. Rosenthal's, with its transparent clocks and weird metal sculptures, Mr. Patton's office boasted the usual trappings of an attorney's office — dark wall paneling, leather sofas, and a massive wooden desk. I gazed at the photographs on the wall of Mr. Patton with senators and governors.

Finally there was a short knock on the door and Lloyd Barber walked in. He brought to mind J. Edgar Hoover. He had the same brooding bulldog face and powerful, stocky body. He was balding, and his hair was gray. He didn't smile as he shook my hand, introduced himself, and lowered his considerable bulk into a chair. He had already been briefed on the situation by Mr. Rosenthal and began without preamble. His voice was hoarse and low.

"I think I can help you, but first I need to know a few things. Tell me more about what you know — where your children are, who they're living with, something about your ex-husband."

"All I know is that the children are living with Federico in his mother's apartment. They're not in school yet, since it's summer vacation now in Bolivia. I don't know what school they'll be going to."

"Do you think the kids'll both be in the same school or in different schools?"

"I don't know. I do know he'll put them in a private school." Only the poor went to public schools in Bolivia. "Most private schools in La Paz are either all-girl or all-boy. They might end up in different schools."

"Do you have any idea which schools he *might* put them in?"

I thought. Federico had once told me they'd attend the German school; it was coeducational. So was the American school. But I knew he didn't have the money for either of them. His next choice would probably be San Calixto, an all-boys Jesuit school downtown and Federico's old alma mater. Maybe he'd put Michael there and put Jane on the other side of town in San Calixto's sister school. I told him this

"How far apart are they?" Lloyd asked.

"Probably a good ten or fifteen miles."

119

Lloyd was silent a moment. "I know this is a difficult question," he began, "but if they're in different schools it might come down to this. If you could get out with only one child, which one would you choose?"

My heart twisted. How could I choose? My funny, affectionate Michael—how could I leave him behind? And Jane—sweet, tenderhearted, intelligent.

It was useless to consider it. I could' never leave one behind. I blinked away the tears that were threatening to spill over.

"I couldn't take just one. If it came to that, I'd leave them both there. Then at least they'd have each other."

Lloyd nodded and moved briskly on to the next issue. "Where is your ex-husband during the day?"

"I don't know. I don't think he has a regular job, but he won't tell me much."

"Is he dangerous? Does he have a gun?"

"No, I don't think he has a gun. At least, he never used to. But I know he wouldn't just stand by and watch if somebody tried to take the kids." The mention of guns made me uneasy. "*If* I decide to do this, I don't want any violence. I don't want anybody to get hurt." Visions of hit men jumping into a park and blasting Federico or his mother flashed through my mind.

"We don't either. It's not smart to get yourself into any more trouble than you have to. In fact, *you* have to be the one who takes the kids. That way, if you get caught, you tell them you're the mother and you're simply taking your children home. It's more legal that way. If somebody else were to grab them, that would be kidnapping."

It was the first time he'd actually used the word "kidnapping." And what did the term "more legal" mean? Something was either legal or it wasn't. We were entering gray territory now. And yet Lloyd had just answered my most pressing question.

I said firmly, "The only way I would consider doing it is if *I* took them."

Lloyd leaned forward, hands clasped in front of him. "I like that answer." He studied my face for a moment.

"If you decide to go through with this, first we'd have to do a feasibility study. I won't even attempt it if I don't think there's a good chance of success. It would probably take a month or so for that. And I would need $15,000 up front, maybe more. If it doesn't look good, then it ends there. No refunds. If it looks good, then we can go on with it."

Fifteen thousand dollars! "How much would the whole thing cost?"

"Ordinarily, I wouldn't take on an assignment like this for less than $100,000. But as a favor to this law firm, I'll do it for expenses only. After the initial fifteen thousand, it would cost a minimum of fifteen thousand more. Plus you'd need to have ten thousand in reserve, just in case. And don't forget there are no guarantees."

He was talking about a minimum of $40,000!

"Have you done anything like this before?" I asked.

"We've extricated people before," he answered carefully. "You can do anything if you have the right connections. But connections have to be paid for."

He surveyed me coolly, then asked, "How much are you willing to sacrifice to get your children back?" I knew he wasn't talking about money anymore.

"I'll do whatever it takes."

"There might be physical hardships — going without comforts, food, sleep. We might have to travel on foot for long distances, with two kids and luggage. And it will be dangerous."

I nodded.

"If we get caught, we could be thrown in prison. And you can bet the U.S. Embassy won't bail us out." His gravelly voice continued, "There won't be any room for error. You have to promise me your complete trust and obedience. You have to do *exactly* as I say, no questions asked."

Complete obedience? To a total stranger? He was asking me to blindly place the lives of myself and my children in his hands, in a foreign country where I would have no one to turn to, no place to go . . . and yet, what choice had I left? Somehow the interview had turned from being a discussion of possibilities into a commitment. I felt swept along. It was all being decided too fast.

"Afterward, if we succeed, it means you'll have to go underground. You'll have to leave town, change your name, and start all over again somewhere else." I swallowed. I already knew that would have to be a part of it.

"Can you do all that?" Lloyd asked. We studied each other across the carpet, his face almost glowering. I met his gaze and nodded slowly, "Yes, I can."

His face relaxed, and for the first time I saw a hint of a smile on it. "You know what? I think you can too."

I told him I'd talk with my father about it over the weekend and get in touch with him the following week.

Afterward, as I drove home, I opened the window and took a deep breath. The warm afternoon air was lightly scented with spring flowers. The breeze coming in the window seemed to fan a dormant spark of hope in me. The very air outside seemed a little brighter and clearer, as if a hazy gray curtain had lifted.

When I called my father and told him about my meeting with Lloyd, he said, "Let's do it." He would be in charge of getting the money together.

I wondered where he would come up with it all. I ticked off the possibilities: there was Courtney, of course. But she couldn't be expected to foot the whole bill. Then there was my brother Tom. He was a surgeon in private practice in Odessa, and he'd offered his help from the beginning. My younger brother John would do what he could. But he'd just bought a house and might not have the resources now. Then there was my grandmother. My brothers and I had always called her "Littie," short for Elizabeth, which was my middle name, too.

Littie owned mineral rights to a small piece of land in West Texas, and a few years ago they had struck oil. The royalties amounted to several thousand dollars a month, or at least it had been that much in the boom times. Boom times had since gone bust, but she still had most of the money, squirreled away in CD's. In spite of her windfall, Littie's modest life-style hadn't changed. She still lived with my Uncle Tom, Daddy's younger brother, in the small frame house she'd lived in as long as I could remember. Now frail and in her eighties, she barely had the strength to talk. But her keen eyes took in everything. I was sure I could count on her to help, too.

The next day Daddy called and told me he'd send a cashier's check for the first $15,000 within the next few days.

Things seemed to be gathering a momentum of

their own. I had a few moments of panic during the next few days. *I need more time to think. Am I being premature? Should I wait for the outcome of the legal process before taking this step?*

There were other fears, too. It bothered me to think that I would be in debt for the rest of my life, with no hope of ever paying it back—not only to Mr. Rosenthal, but now to members of my own family.

And what if, after all, we failed? All that money for nothing. And nothing to fall back on, not even the hope of the Bolivian courts. There would be no recourse at all if this venture failed. I'd simply have to resign myself to never seeing my children again.

Ironically, it was almost as frightening to think about the future if we succeeded—starting all over again, raising Jane and Michael alone, always looking over my shoulder in fear. I had barely been able to make ends meet with child support coming in. How would I ever manage without it? And what about Federico? Could I live with myself knowing I'd taken away all he had, even his children? I'd be saddled with that guilt for the rest of my life.

Daddy reasoned with me. "You shouldn't feel guilty. He's the one who started this. Besides, you're not depriving him of the kids. If he really wanted to see them, he could come back here and serve his time in jail. He could live here if he wanted to be with them." Still it bothered me. The burdens that went along with winning made it tempting to forfeit the game altogether.

Meanwhile, only my immediate family and Mr. Rosenthal knew what was afoot—not only for the security of the operation but to preserve Lloyd's anonymity. Mr. Rosenthal's involvement was to remain a secret too. I couldn't even tell Susan or Kathy.

My daily activities took on a temporary feel. I started seeing everything through different eyes. Friends were more dear, sunsets more beautiful. What I'd be leaving became all the more precious. If I succeeded, I wouldn't see them again. And if I failed and didn't get my kids back? I didn't want to consider that possibility. I could barely contain my excitement and anticipation. After all the months of depending on others to do everything, I was finally going to do something *myself*.

Chapter Nine

As soon as Lloyd got the initial $15,000 he sent someone to Bolivia to do whatever mysterious things had to be done to set up the operation. He would call me twice a week with a report and we met twice in a local restaurant. But he told me very little. His own information was sketchy, he said; his phone calls to Bolivia were channeled through a hotel switchboard, and they had to be careful about what they said.

At first, Lloyd thought it could be pulled off over the Easter holidays. His plan was to take the children across Lake Titicaca into Peru. Lake Titicaca was the highest lake in the world and one of the biggest. Somewhere in the middle of it an imaginary line divided Peru from Bolivia, but on certain jagged peninsulas the boundary was on the land itself. It was on one of these that the pretty little town of Copacabana nestled. It was a popular tourist attraction, mainly because it was the launching point for boats bound for the Island of the Sun and the Island of the Moon, historically important sites in the history of the ancient Incas.

More important to Bolivians, however, was the fact that the town cathedral sheltered the Virgin of Copacabana, a diminutive, gem-encrusted statue of the Virgin Mary widely believed to possess miraculous powers. She serenely looked down on the worshippers in the old church from a little alcove high above the altar. Baroque decorations bathed in 18-carat gold surrounded her from floor to ceiling. Every Easter swarms of pilgrims arrived from all over Peru and Bolivia to pay homage to her and to ask for favors. Many of these pilgrims came on foot as a sort of reenactment of Christ's walk along the Via Dolorosa, traveling for days and camping at night on the frosty *altiplano*.

What interested Lloyd, however, was not the Virgin, but the fact that at Eastertime, border controls would be lax. Because of the sheer numbers of people crossing back and forth, it would be a perfect opportunity to slip the children into Peru undetected.

But there were some hitches. Lloyd didn't count on the one thing you could count on in Bolivia, which was that you *couldn't* count on anything. As Easter neared, he learned from his man in Bolivia that the rainy season was in full swing. The only road from La Paz to Copacabana was washed out. On top of that, there was some sort of civil unrest going on—Lloyd didn't know exactly what—something about miners going on strike and marching in the streets of La Paz. A general strike was in effect, too. I'd lived in Bolivia long enough to know what that meant: everything would come to a grinding halt. There'd be no buses or taxis and no gasoline. What little food there was would be jealously hoarded by shopkeepers. Schools and businesses would close, and airports would be empty. Lloyd said we'd just have to wait for conditions to be more favorable.

I still didn't know exactly what my role would be. If Lloyd had a plan in mind, he was telling me precious little about it. His responses to my questions were purposefully vague. But his instructions as to preparations were precise.

"First, buy plane tickets from McAllen to La Paz for yourself *and* for the children, round trip. That way it looks like you brought them into Bolivia with you. You might get by with taking them out again — you are simply tourists returning home. I want you to do this: make the reservations, buy the tickets and pick them up, then cancel the reservations."

"Why?"

"I don't want them to be on a computer. Your ex-husband might be having somebody monitor flight reservations for him."

I nodded. If only I had thought of having *his* reservations monitored, I wouldn't be here right now.

"When it's time to leave, just show up at the

airport. When they can't find your reservations, tell them they made a mistake. You'll have the tickets as proof that you were booked on the flight."

I was dubious. "What if the flight is full and they won't let me on?"

"Be insistent. Reservations get canceled. It happens all the time. They know that." He continued, "I want you to be packed and ready to go at a moment's notice. Get together all the legal papers and the Spanish translations and make about a dozen copies of each. Get extra photographs of the children, passport size. And buy a wig for yourself to wear down there."

I was furiously taking notes. A wig?

"Pack light. You don't want to be weighed down with anything unnecessary. We probably won't be there longer than forty-eight hours, anyway. Don't take anything you can't leave behind. Wear shoes you can run in."

"Will I be flying down alone?"

"I'll be going too, but not at the same time." Mr. Rosenthal would be relieved to hear that. He figured that Lloyd would have more of a personal stake in my safety if he was there too.

Later in the month, I started collecting the things I'd need for the trip. I dusted off my old blue suitcase and opened it on the floor. Each day a few more items went into it. First was the thick sheaf of legal documents and photos of the children, along with their birth certificates. I shopped for two lightweight duffle bags and folded them into a corner of the suitcase. I planned to stuff whatever I needed for the return trip into the duffle bags and leave the cumbersome suitcase behind in Bolivia. On the plane I decided to wear a comfortably baggy pair of jeans and a long-sleeved knit shirt. I'd take an extra sweater and light jacket for La Paz. I packed a nice blouse and a pair of slacks in case I should need to be more dressed up for, say, a visit to the consulate. My long johns could double as pajamas. A couple of changes of underthings completed my travel wardrobe.

For Jane and Michael I packed extra sweaters for the cold Bolivian highlands and new blue jeans a size larger than what they'd worn five months ago — better too big than too small. For Michael I packed a cap to pull down over his head, and for Jane a hooded windbreaker to hide her light hair. Into the suitcase went a couple of their old favorite toys, and a brightly wrapped new toy for each.

Then I bought a wig. It was long, curly and almost black — completely different from my straight blonde hair. With the wig on, I'd blend in with the dark-haired masses, and from the side you could hardly see my face.

Lloyd's last instruction was harder to comply

with: passports for the children. When they were infants I'd gotten United States passports for them in La Paz. I had renewed Jane's only a year ago, after the five-year expiration period had passed, but her new passport had disappeared. I didn't know whether Federico had taken it or it had gotten lost in our last move. I still had Michael's, though. From its pages a sleepy six-week-old baby gazed into the camera. But his passport would expire in April, which was fast approaching.

The problem now was getting new photographs for the passport applications. They had to be recent—less than a year old—and there had to be two of them, made from the same negative. And, of course, they had to be passport size.

All of these requirements posed problems. The only passport pictures I had of the children were over a year old. I didn't have the negatives, either. In fact, only one photograph had been developed from a negative; the other two were Polaroid prints, which were no longer accepted by the passport agency.

Back in December, I had tried to get new passport pictures by attempting to find the original studio where Jane's photograph had been taken. I thought that they might have kept the negative. One afternoon I drove up and down the shabby streets of downtown McAllen—which were more reminiscent of a Mexican town than an American one—and finally found the studio. But the studio owner shook his head. He had not kept the negative. Then I moved on to the studio where Michael's Polaroid photos had been taken the year before. The woman at the front desk glanced at the photographs I gave her.

"We don't use negatives for passport photos."

"I know," I said, "but I thought you might have kept extra copies or something."

"No, but . . ." she examined the photos more carefully. "I remember these children." She looked up. "They were in here a few months ago, in September, I think. They were having visa photographs made, for somewhere in South America. Their father brought them in."

Another piece in the puzzle had fallen into place, only it was a few months too late.

Next, I called around to find a lab that could make duplicate prints from the photos I had. In the entire Rio Grande Valley there was only one with that capability. I had to choose the right photo of Jane for the lab to copy. I couldn't remember which one I'd sent in for her renewal passport the year before. Would the U.S. Passport Agency notice if I sent in the same one? I'd just have to take that chance.

Making the duplicates was a process that took more time and effort than I had imagined. After three weeks the photographs came back fuzzy and too large. I took them back. After several trials and errors, the lab had produced copies that were the right size and reasonably clear. I hoped that the passport agency wouldn't spot the fact that they were copies. I took the applications and photographs to the local passport office. I knew it was against their policy to issue a passport to someone who wasn't present in person to apply for it. But if the passports were for children, a parent could apply without the children being physically present. The clerk accepted the applications and photos without comment.

I didn't hear anything until March 8, when I got a phone call from the regional passport agency in Houston. The voice on the phone wanted to know why Jane's photograph was the same one I'd sent in for her renewal passport eighteen months earlier. I had chosen wrong.

"She's not in town right now so I couldn't have a new picture taken." I tried to sound smooth and confident. "She's visiting her grandmother," I added. She wanted to know why I couldn't have her picture taken wherever her grandmother was. I mumbled something about having plans to travel soon and not having time to have new pictures made.

"Well," she said crisply. "We can't issue a passport with this picture. If you can send in a recent photograph of her, we'll reconsider."

I took the other photograph of Jane to the lab. By then I was a familiar and not very welcome face around there. Three more weeks passed before the picture was ready. I was running out of time. At the post office I tried to hide my unease as I produced the photos. The agent glanced at them, then at me. Nervously, she told me that she could not accept my applications for either child unless I brought them in with me. They were on to me. I argued with her briefly, but she shook her head.

"I'm sorry, those are orders from Houston. If you want to talk to the director there, I'll give you his phone number." I called Houston from her desk. The director was adamant: no children, no passports. In desperation I told him the truth: I couldn't bring the children with me because they had been kidnapped by their father and taken to South America. I was working on getting legal custody of them through the Bolivian courts.

"In that case, after you have custody, you can get the passports there in Bolivia at the U.S. Consulate."

I didn't *want* to do it in Bolivia, I argued. I wanted to be able to fly down, gather them up, and leave without dillydallying. The director was unmoved. With tears of frustration I hung up. Several pairs of curious eyes watched as I gathered the rejected applications and marched out of the room.

Why wouldn't my own government help me? I could understand that rules were there to prevent abuses of the system. Yet when it had *proof* that a crime against one of its own citizens had been committed, that a foreigner had flagrantly violated its laws, my country still refused to bend the rules for me. What bureaucratic pettiness! I fumed. That same day Mr. Rosenthal called up a lawyer at the passport office in Washington, D.C., to explain that the children had been kidnapped and that I needed to have their passports before I went to Bolivia.

There was a slight pause, and the attorney said dryly, "What she's planning to do is to kidnap them."

"No," Mr. Rosenthal said patiently, "*He* kidnapped them. She's going down to reclaim what's rightfully hers." But it was no use. They wouldn't budge, not even when Mr. Rosenthal got the local Congressman to intervene. I would have to get the passports in Bolivia somehow.

By early April I had everything ready. There was nothing to do but wait for the go-ahead from Lloyd. Every time the phone rang I leaped out of my skin. If it was Lloyd he'd ask for David. I was supposed to say he had the wrong number, then go to a designated pay phone nearby and wait for him to call back. It seemed silly to go through such elaborate precautions. But he was the one calling the shots.

Meanwhile, Jane's birthday on April 12 was fast approaching. Michael's had already come and

136

gone, on January 17. He was five years old. I had mailed him a pair of Superman house slippers and wondered what kind of party he'd had, who had come, what they'd eaten, what games they'd played. Probably no games at all. Bolivians had very traditional ways of doing things, and birthdays were no exception. Parents would invite their own adult friends and relatives and serve a formal afternoon tea. For the children there would sometimes be a piñata.

I had my own sentimental little traditions, like the annual birthday letter. By the time April 11 arrived, my hopes of being with Jane on her birthday seemed as remote as ever. I wrote her a birthday letter, not to mail but to tuck away, to help me remember how she was when I saw her last:

Dear Jane,

Tomorrow is your birthday, and I won't be there to see your eyes shining in the glow of the seven candles. I worry about how you are taking it all. You are so tenderhearted. Even as a toddler, you couldn't stand to see any creature hurt. I finally gave up trying to get you to watch "Charlotte's Web." The minute you saw the pig and the ax being carried off to the barn you'd cover your eyes and demand that I turn it off. You'd offer your cookie to any mangy hound on the street. In

137

your nursery school you were always the one to befriend the little girl that nobody else liked.

Your own feelings are easily hurt. Slights roll off Michael like water off a duck, but you take them to heart. With you I wanted to be a mother hen hovering over her baby chick, but I forced myself to hover a few feet away. If I seemed unfeeling at times, it was because I wanted you to learn to fend for yourself. Now more than ever how I wish I could cover you with my wings and protect you from all the little hailstones that will sting you as you grow!

I wonder how tall you have grown, what your favorite toys are, who you play with. Do you say your prayers at night, do you have enough warm clothes and a pretty dress or two, do you miss me? It's hard to set aside my longing and be objective about what's best for you. But I keep coming to the conclusion that you and Michael belong here with me. You both are precious to me and I will never give up.

Love,
Mommy

Lloyd's voice was terse. "Be in Bolivia by Monday. It's time." My stomach fluttered. The moment

Federico and I met and began dating in the summer of 1975 when we were both students at the University of Texas at Austin.

We traveled to California in the summer of 1977, and made a side trip to Tijuana, where this picture was taken.

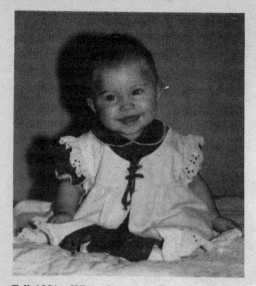

Fall 1981 — When Jane was five months old, we made our first visit home to Austin. She was such a happy and friendly baby!

Fall 1981 — Federico joined Jane and me for the last couple of weeks of our stay in Austin. Here we're standing in front of the building on the University of Texas campus where we met in a French class.

La Paz, March 1983 — Jane, almost two, holding her six-week-old brother Michael.

La Paz, March 1983 — Federico, Jane, and six-week-old Michael in our house in La Paz.

La Paz, 1984 — Jane and Michael were always close. Here they were playing at home, taking turns pushing each other on a hobby horse.

La Paz, 1984—The street we lived on from 1982 to 1985, as seen from the second floor balcony of our rented house.

La Paz, 1984—Food Aid International operated breakfast programs for poor children in this slum neighborhood on the outskirts of La Paz, near the airport.

McAllen, Texas, summer 1986—In spite of the smiles, our marriage was in trouble when this family portrait was taken.

McAllen, Texas, fall 1986—"Granddaddy" (my father) with Jane and Michael during a visit with us.

McAllen, Texas, spring 1987—This photo of Jane and Michael was taken at our church in McAllen for the membership directory.

McAllen, Texas, October 31, 1987—I took this picture of Jane and Michael in their Halloween costumes just before we went to their school's Halloween carnival. Thirteen days later, Federico kidnapped them.

McAllen, Texas, fall 1987 — Kathy Rupard was Mr. Rosenthal's secretary and my friend.

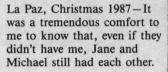

La Paz, Christmas 1987 — It was a tremendous comfort to me to know that, even if they didn't have me, Jane and Michael still had each other.

La Paz, April 26, 1988 — Michael performed in
the school fiesta at Amor de Dios school.
Federico took this picture, and the following
one of Jane, as I stood watching from a nearby
window.

La Paz, April 26,
1988 — Jane watched as
Michael's class performed a
native dance from Tarija in
the school fiesta. Three
days later we were reunited.

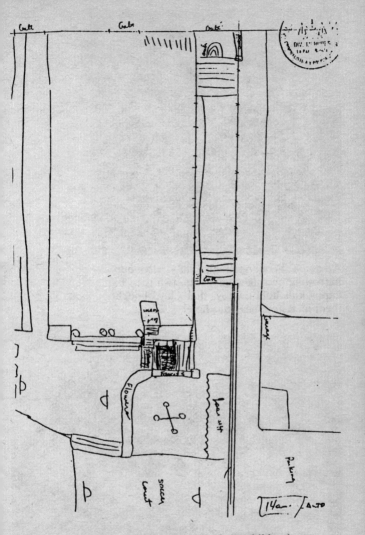

La Paz, April 1988 — I drew this map of the children's school, Amor de Dios, in the apartment next door, where the Bolivian police found it a few days after we escaped.

Arequipa, Peru, April 30, 1988 — After our harrowing overnight train ride, two tired but happy kids hold the toys that Lloyd bought them in a store near our hotel.

Arequipa, Peru, May 1, 1988 — from left to right — Michael, Jane, Bob, Lloyd and I (in my wig) at breakfast before leaving for the airport.

Arequipa, Peru, May 1, 1988 — The children pose in front of the altar where a few minutes earlier Jane was praying for a safe trip home.

Arequipa, Peru, May 1, 1988 — clockwise — Jane, me, Bob, Lloyd, and Michael in the Arequipa airport before flying to Lima.

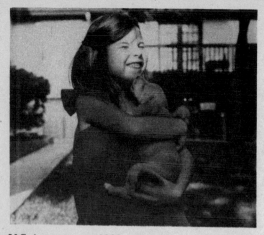

U.S.A., summer 1988—Jane got a lick from a neighbor's friendly puppy. By now we had moved and started over again in the United States.

U.S.A., summer 1989—Jane, Michael, and I a year after our South American odyssey, back to a normal life again—or as normal as life ever gets!

had finally arrived. My mind was flooded with questions. Was Lloyd flying down with me? What was I supposed to do once I got there? Was someone going to meet me? But I knew by then not to ask questions. Now, as always, he told me only what he wanted me to know.

"Go to the El Dorado Hotel when you get there. And remember, once you're in Bolivia, no phone calls to the States."

After Lloyd left, I knocked on Mr. Rosenthal's door and went in. A haze of cigar smoke hung about his desk, where he sat with his feet propped up, an impish grin on his face. "What's up, kid?" His phone rang. I waited impatiently for the call to finish, then told him, "D Day has arrived."

His face drooped perceptibly. Whatever happened, our strange and interesting relationship would be different. I would be leaving McAllen, whether I got the children back or not. For the past nine months, he had been my chief hand-holder and cheerleader, someone to whom I could say anything and know he'd still accept me. Someone who, when I *didn't* say what was on my mind, knew at once and would chide, "Come on, Cass. This is Uncle Doug. You can't fool me." I had come to care for him in a deep and special way. I would miss him very much.

Friday, my last day at Patton & Jones, arrived quickly. I felt buoyant with hope, happier than I'd been in months. In a few days I'd be reunited with my children! I was convinced of it. Yet there was a sadness to the day, too. I would disappear without being able to say good-bye to my friends. No one but Mr. Rosenthal knew what was afoot. I longed to take my special friends aside and tell them how much I'd miss them. Instead I made a point of spending a little time visiting with each one that Friday, and whispered a silent good-bye as I walked away.

The Recovery

Chapter Ten

Monday, April 18, 1988

I was in Miami. Plastic flamingos stood in the corners of the hotel coffee shop, and the ceiling was festooned with twinkling white lights that would've been more at home on a Christmas tree. I'd flown in from McAllen the night before and spent the night in this rather shabby and overpriced hotel near the Miami International Airport. I glanced at my watch and gulped down the rest of my coffee. The airport shuttle would be leaving soon. I climbed aboard the van with a few other passengers and we rode a few blocks to the airport.

It was bustling with an interesting hodgepodge of humankind. There were the Miami types, bronzed men dressed in white cotton and gold chains, standing in line with Orthodox Jews wearing broad-brimmed black hats and earlocks. I passed a knot of Cubans talking in clipped Spanish, and farther on, Jamaicans laughing and shaking their dreadlocks at some private joke. And, of course, the international businessmen, indistinguishable in their generic dark business suits.

At the ticket counter I was put on the flight to La Paz without any problems, in spite of the fact that my reservations had been "lost." After walking the equivalent of several football fields past ticket counters for what seemed like every airline in the world, I approached the gate where my flight was to depart.

I spotted Lloyd immediately. He was wearing his pearl gray suit and sunglasses, and was seated in the waiting section of the departure gate. So he *had* come! He seemed to be looking in my direction, but he gave no sign of recognition. I took his cue and walked on by. After a few minutes he took the seat next to mine and began an innocuous conversation as if we were strangers. After a while he asked casually, "Do you have all the documents?"

"Yes."

"And the extra money?" I nodded. He was referring to the extra $5000 dollars in cash that I was supposed to keep with me, "in case you get separated from the rest of us," he'd said. The money made a sizable bundle in my purse, even in $50 bills. For weeks I'd cached it in my apartment in a dozen different hiding places where I hoped a burglar wouldn't think to look. Once it was hidden under the rags in the mop bucket under the kitchen sink. It was with great relief when I'd come home from work each day and find the money still there, and double relief that I could remember where I'd last put it. I held my purse close to my side.

"What about your wig?"

"It's in here." I patted my carry-on bag.

"You should've worn it," Lloyd said shortly. Then he moved away. I studied my fellow passengers. So far I didn't recognize anyone. Not all the passengers were going to La Paz, though. It was the last stop on an itinerary that included Panama City and Lima, Peru.

As luck would have it, our travel plans coincided with the FAA's crackdown on Eastern Airlines. Every outbound Eastern flight was required to undergo an FAA inspection before being cleared for takeoff. Shortly after we boarded our flight, the pilot announced it had been grounded: inspectors had found a mechanical problem. We were herded off the plane and down the concourse to another boarding gate. There we waited for several hours, only to be told that this plane, too, had been grounded after inspection.

At that point all the Bolivian-bound passengers were reassigned to flights on the Bolivian airlines, Lloyd Aereo Boliviano, or LAB for short. It would leave around ten P.M. and arrive in La Paz the following morning. Lloyd decided to go on to La Paz on LAB, but I opted to stay with Eastern, even though it meant waiting two more days—until Wednesday—for the next flight to La Paz. It was just too risky to fly LAB—most of the passengers would be Bolivian. If one of them recognized

145

me, it could get back to Federico.

One other passenger, though he was Bolivian, chose to forgo the tiring overnight LAB flight and stay with Eastern. Mr. Sanchez and I were thrown together as partners in frustration all Monday afternoon and into the evening as we tried to retrieve our luggage, which had been transferred to the LAB flight along with everyone else's from our Eastern flight, before it got sent on to La Paz and certain oblivion. Mr. Sanchez was very helpful in dealing with the LAB airline agents, and they eventually produced our luggage. I accepted a sandwich he kindly bought me. It was the only food I'd eaten since breakfast in the flamingo room, but I politely turned down his offer to stay at his beach condo until Wednesday.

Instead I spent the next two nights at a luxurious Miami hotel, courtesy of Eastern Airlines. With two days on my hands and nothing to do, I loaded up on crossword puzzle books and started the Dorothy Sayers mystery I'd brought. I also bought a rather daring swimsuit in the hotel boutique — the only suit in my size — and unwisely spent all day Tuesday dozing by the pool. The idea was to enhance my disguise by tanning my skin to a darker shade. But the result was a fiery red and extremely painful sunburn — I could have been the poster girl for Solarcaine. That night I went down to the hotel restaurant for dinner. A lounge was at the entrance to the restaurant, and men in white suits were circling like sharks. I beat a hasty retreat to a cafe around the corner. It wouldn't be the last time I would wonder if I was out of my depth.

The next morning I was up by seven o'clock. Carefully I pinned up my hair, then tugged the wig down over my head. The mirror told me that I had been transformed into a gypsy. I felt exotic, wild, and conspicuously phony. Surely everyone would see right through me. I watched the clerk as I paid my bill at the desk. He didn't seem to notice anything amiss. Of course, he was probably used to seeing much stranger things than a woman wearing a wig. On the airport shuttle someone asked me if I was a model. Maybe the wig wasn't so bad after all. I told him I was a journalist.

This time our plane made it off the ground. It would be a long flight: twelve hours, with layovers in Panama City and Lima. I saw Mr. Sanchez a few rows ahead of me and watched as he scanned the faces of his fellow passengers. His eyes rested on me for a moment and a look of puzzlement passed over them. With a slight pang of guilt at repaying his kindness in such a way, I gave him what I hoped was a disinterested glance and looked away. I felt his gaze on me several times during the flight, but to my relief he never spoke.

I remained constantly aware of my fellow passengers. Was that one paying more than casual attention to me? I tensed up. Did he recognize me? Did he know Federico? During layovers I stayed in my seat.

147

Finally, at about 10:30 P.M., the plane began to circle above the La Paz airport. At two miles of altitude, it was the highest airport in the world. A local joke was that planes didn't descend to land there, they flew upward. Shivering, I pulled on a sweater and jacket. Although it was springtime in Texas, winter was approaching in the Southern Hemisphere. Anyway, here on the high Andean plateau, it was chilly year round.

We disembarked directly onto the tarmac — South American airports didn't boast the luxury of weatherproof boarding tunnels. And instead of the shopping mall atmosphere of the Miami air terminal, with its plush carpet and piped-in music, the La Paz airport was bare, stark and cold.

We lined up at the immigration checkpoint while grim-faced military police examined our papers. I scanned the waiting crowd, wondering if anybody would be there to meet me. Lloyd had told me that if no one met me at the airport, I was to take a taxi directly to the El Dorado Hotel. No one stepped forward, so suitcase in hand, I made my way outside to get a taxi. The somber flat-featured faces of native Bolivians surrounded me. I felt like an Amazon — at 5'9" I towered over nearly all of them.

Outside, I chose among the cab drivers clamoring for my patronage and squeezed into the backseat of a dilapidated taxi. Soon I was joined by two other Americans. We began the long descent into La Paz, which lay several hundred feet down the mountain from the airport. Seen from the air, La Paz looked ike a huge crevice in the flat plain between the two Andean mountain ranges, the eastern and western Cordilleras. On the road, at night, it was like driving into a huge bowl of stars. The twinkling lights hid the ugliness of the hillside slums we were passing through. Looming in the distance like a sentinel guarding the city stood snow-peaked Mount Illimani. During my last year in Bolivia, on New Year's Day 1985, a Braniff airplane had crashed into Illimani. Blinding blizzards and steep slopes had thwarted all recovery attempts, and the bodies and wreckage still lay entombed in the ice near its peak. Illimani was a constant, brooding presence over the city.

The young couple in the taxi asked me what I was doing in Bolivia. My story was ready: I was a journalist, on assignment for the *Los Angeles Times,* I added as an afterthought, and hoped neither of them was from Los Angeles and had an uncle or aunt who worked on the paper. When they asked what had brought me to La Paz, I explained that I couldn't divulge what my mysterious mission was or even where I'd be staying. They were fascinated. They probably thought my assignment had something to do with the drug trade—most people thought of cocaine when they thought of Bolivia at all. Or perhaps they thought I was there to cover the Pope's visit; he was due to arrive in three weeks.

Around the last bend in the road lay the city proper. Buildings dating back to Spanish colonial times rose on either side of narrow, brick-paved streets. North Americans sometimes assume that all of South America is like the United States' nearest Latin neighbor, Mexico. But Bolivia is a world apart. Where Mexico is colorful, noisy, and festive, Bolivia is gray, somber, and mysterious. Mexicans are garrulous, outgoing, aggressive; people from La Paz are fatalistic, stubborn, remote. The native Indians from the La Paz area, the Aymaras, are descendants of the only tribe that was never conquered by the Incas and incorporated into their empire. Even now they resist all attempts at modernization and cling stubbornly to their old ways and beliefs.

It was nearly 11 P.M. as we entered the city, but the streets still swarmed with people, mostly Aymara Indians dressed in their traditional garb. The women wore several layers of velvet skirts—the number of skirts they wore indicated their wealth. On their heads perched derby hats, and they wore fringed shawls around their shoulders. Some carried rosy-cheeked babies tied to their backs with colorful, hand-loomed blankets. The men were thinner and more plainly dressed in dark pants and jackets and wool caps with earflaps. Their faces wore an expression as dull as the streets around them. Beggars and peddlers slowed traffic on the sidewalks. Braided urchins no bigger than Michael begged passersby to buy candy or gum.

My taxi companions were disgorged in the Indian district near the San Francisco Cathedral, where they would find humble lodgings listed in their

"South America on $5 and $10 A Day" guidebook, places with concrete floors and hot showers at 6 A.M. The driver continued through downtown. The main street turned into a boulevard lined with flowers, benches, and equestrian statues of Bolivian heroes. We passed the elegant Plaza Hotel and the university, a single tall building draped with banners proclaiming socialist slogans.

The driver pulled up in front of the El Dorado Hotel. Before I was out of the taxi, I saw Lloyd approaching. He was with another man I didn't recognize.

"Cecilia?" Lloyd stepped forward. My alias, Lloyd had decreed back in Texas, would be Cecilia Jones. He introduced "Raul," who for all the world looked like an insurance salesman on vacation. Paunchy and balding, maybe in his late forties, "Raul" had blue eyes that twinkled as he grinned and shook my hand.

"The El Dorado is full," Lloyd said. "We'll go to the Copacabana Hotel down the street." He motioned me back into the taxi and both men squeezed in beside me. Lloyd surveyed me with a grin.

"You know, Cecilia," he said in his heavy-handed way, "that wig is very becoming. I've always had a thing for Carmen." I was so happy and relieved to be with someone I knew that I grinned right back.

The Copacabana was an old streetfront hotel like the El Dorado. Inside, the clerk shoved an immigration form across the desk at me. I was puzzled. I knew that in Bolivia everyone who registered in a hotel had to show a passport or a Bolivian I.D. card. These records were then sent to the Ministry of the Interior, probably as a means of keeping tabs on foreigners. Hadn't Lloyd known about this and made provisions for it ahead of time? I didn't dare ask now. I couldn't read Raul's face as he stood silently next to me. I fished my passport out of my purse and the clerk copied my name and passport number onto the form. A red capped porter grabbed my bags and we all ascended in silence up the creaking elevator.

As soon as we were inside my room, Lloyd scolded me. "You weren't supposed to sign the register. Didn't you see me signaling you?"

"No."

"Raul was supposed to sign the register, not you." I felt properly abashed. I had been here only twenty minutes and had already screwed up.

"Well, we'll see what we can do to fix that," Lloyd said gruffly. "Do you need us to get you anything?"

My throat felt dry, and I knew the tap water wasn't potable. "I could use some water."

"We'll bring you some and be back in a while." They left.

I looked around the spartan room. It was quite a change from the luxury of the hotel in Miami. Cramped and dimly lit, it contained a sagging single bed, bare floors with a threadbare rug, and no heat. I followed the sound of a constantly running

152

toilet into the bathroom. The shower ran only cold water. I then ran the tap. Rusty cold water spurted out. Suddenly I felt very tired and stretched out on the bed. Not a very comfortable place, but after all, I would be here for only a couple of days. My heart quickened at the thought—in two days I might be leaving Bolivia with Jane and Michael. As soon as there was an opportunity I would ask Lloyd and Raul about them.

In a few minutes Lloyd returned with several bottles of mineral water. He perched his bulk on the bed and without preface launched into a briefing on the situation. My heart sank as I listened.

"I'm going to tell it like it is. Your children never leave that apartment of your mother-in-law's except to go to school at Amor de Dios. Federico drives them to school himself every morning. That's the *only* place they ever go. We've never seen any show of affection or warmth between Federico and the children. We've never seen them smile. They get into his car like little robots and they get out like little robots. He walks them up to the school and watches them go through an iron gate into the schoolyard." By now my teeth were clenched so tightly together that my jaws had begun to ache.

Lloyd went on, "In all my experience, I've never seen a situation with so few options. It's marginal, very marginal." My teeth began to chatter now, and my eyes filled with tears.

Lloyd demanded irritably, "Why are you crying?"

153

"It sounds like such a bleak existence," I whispered.

"Bleak isn't the word for it, my dear," he said more kindly. "You have reason to cry for that. But remember, you are the key player in this, and you've got to hold yourself together."

I nodded. Outside the window, music blared from a cafe across the street. The reflection of a neon light flashed on and off the wall of the room. There was a rap on the door. Lloyd stood and opened it.

"I've got us a room at the Sheraton," Raul said breathlessly, closing the door behind him. "I got your hotel registration back, too, and tore it up."

After gulping a bottle of the water Lloyd had brought, we gathered my two small bags and stood once more at the elevator. Raul winked and said, "You've got beautiful kids. I've been watching them for over a month now. They seem to be real close. They're always holding hands." I blinked back tears again. At least they had each other.

I cleared my throat. "Lloyd said they never smile." Please tell me differently, I silently begged, but Raul avoided my eyes and said nothing. My heart dropped along with the elevator.

The polished floors and huge spiky chandelier of the Sheraton Hotel lobby were almost comforting in their familiarity. I'd been there many times to partake of an American-style breakfast of eggs and pancakes, or to buy the latest copy of *Time* or *Newsweek* in its shop. Raul took my luggage and proceeded to the desk to register the room in his name, while Lloyd and I took the elevator to my fifth-floor room. It was spacious and comfortable, with thick carpeting and a large picture window looking out over the city.

Before they left me for the night, I learned that Raul's real name was Bob Kreiler. That certainly fit him better than Raul. They told me they'd be back in the morning and warned me not to open the door to anybody.

My body was weary but my mind was racing. Was I up to what lay before me? And when would I find out what that was? Did they have a plan ready? When would we carry it out? What was my role to be? Before I fell into a heavy sleep, I prayed the same prayer I had been praying for months: Dear God, watch over my children. If it's Your will, give them back to me. If not, help me somehow to accept that.

Chapter Eleven

Thursday, April 21, 1988

I got up early and was bathed and dressed by 8 A.M. It would be my second day to wear the wig. To pass the time, I did crosswords and wrote in my journal. By ten o'clock no one had shown up and I was starving. I dialed room service and in rusty Spanish ordered breakfast. It couldn't hurt, I reasoned — in a hotel this big, the waiter wouldn't know that a woman was occupying the room that a man named Bob had registered for . . . or would he?

I felt lightheaded, both from hunger and from the effects of the higher altitude. The waiter arrived and laid out quite a spread: a basket of rolls and breads, jams and butter, juice, and *café con leche,* thick Bolivian coffee made with steamed milk. Shortly after I laid down my napkin, Lloyd showed up. He glanced at the untidy table and reprimanded me for ordering the food. Embarrassed, I apologized. Maybe I wasn't taking this cloak-and-dagger stuff seriously enough. He told me it was foolish to take a chance, to assume people wouldn't notice things.

"How did you pay for it? You don't have any Bolivian money yet," he asked.

"Uh, I charged it to the room." I felt like a kid caught with his hand in the cookie jar.

"Did you sign anything?" he demanded.

"Well, I signed the tab. I just scribbled down some initials, as illegibly as I could." After all, I didn't know Bob's last name. But I figured the hotel people would think nothing of the scrawled initials. Bolivians seemed to take great pains to create individualized and totally unreadable signatures.

"Don't do it again," Lloyd scolded. "Don't *ever* do anything unless we tell you to. We'll take care of the food and whatever else you need."

He went on briskly, "We're moving you out of this room today anyway. There's a suite on the other side of the hotel, with a sitting room adjoining it. That way we'll be closer to you and we'll have space to make plans. If a maid comes to clean the room, you can switch to the other room. That way nobody has to know you were ever here."

For the second time since my arrival in La Paz, then, I was moved to another room.

As soon as I entered my new quarters I went to the window, which faced south. From there I had a clear view of the apartment building where Federico and the children were living with Nila, some three or four blocks down the street from the hotel. I counted up from the ground to the fifteenth floor, where her three-bedroom apartment occupied half the floor. I

157

knew her living room was on the other side of the building, overlooking the circular Isabel la Catolica Plaza. I remembered the room clearly, having eaten many meals there and sat many times on her formal velvet sofa. The room was furnished with a mixture of handmade Bolivian furniture and quite a few artifacts that Nila and her husband had collected in Asia: solid brass tables from Afghanistan, urns and carvings, a painting of a Burmese dancer, and a huge Persian rug.

On the side of the building facing the Sheraton would be the TV room and one of the bedrooms. I squinted. The curtains seemed to be drawn. My heart thumped. At that very minute my children might be sitting in one of those rooms behind those curtains. Lloyd came up beside me.

"I'll bring you some binoculars later and you can watch the windows." I nodded, unable to speak.

After I had gotten settled into the suite, I met the third member of the team: Guy. A dapper man in his sixties, Guy looked out of place in gray La Paz in his white slacks and short-sleeved tropical shirt. Apparently no one had briefed him on local weather conditions.

Lloyd said proudly, "Don't you think Guy could pass for your father? I thought we might run into a situation where that would come in handy." I looked dubiously at Guy. We both had big grins, squarish jaws, and light skin and eyes. But Guy had a slight build and was much shorter than I. He smiled kindly and shook my hand, saying softly, "Don't worry. We're going to get your kids back."

Moments later, Lloyd locked the door between the rooms, shutting me in my half of the suite. Suddenly the room felt empty and cold. The Sheraton was supposed to have central heating, but after a search of the room I could find nothing that resembled a heater or a thermostat. I put on an extra sweater and slipped under the bedcovers for warmth. I lay there listening to the murmur of voices through the adjoining door. I felt completely left out of things. Lloyd kept telling me that the success of the operation hinged on me, yet they were telling me very little of what was really going on. It was frustrating. What did those three gringos know about Bolivia? I had lived here for almost seven years, I thought indignantly, and yet they weren't confiding in me, much less turning to me for information.

My head throbbed and my stomach churned. I recognized the signs of altitude sickness, known as *soroche* by natives and savvy tourists. There was no cure except time, rest, and perhaps a dose of coca tea. Soon it became too much of an effort to hold my eyes open, and I slept.

I was awakened in the afternoon by a knock on the adjoining door. Lloyd had ordered a huge meal for me — four meals, in fact, and he now wheeled them in on a cart.

"This ought to hold you until tomorrow, he said. "There'll be no need for you to repeat your foolishness of this morning." He left me alone again, and I gratefully dug in. The hot soup was delicious. It was made with *chuno,* nasty-looking black potatoes that Indian farmers spread outside on the *altiplano* for days where they froze at night and dehydrated during the day under the fierce sun. The wrinkled, discolored lumps that resulted were quite tasty in spite of their appearance, and could be prepared in a number of ways.

Lloyd, Bob, and Guy were about to leave on some unnamed mission. Before going, Lloyd gave me instructions to call Dr. Castillo, my Bolivian attorney. He wanted to know what our legal status was before proceeding further. If the Bolivian Supreme Court had signed the papers granting me custody, we would be on a much better footing should we get caught trying to leave the country with Jane and Michael. He reminded me not to tell Dr. Castillo that I was in Bolivia.

When I called, Dr. Castillo gave me his usual assurances: everything was fine, and he was certain that I would get my children back.

"What about the court orders? Have they been signed yet?" I asked in Spanish.

"Oh, Catereen," he said regretfully, "I was going to fly to Sucre, and you know what happened? I got sick!" His voice was deep and reassuring. "I have been very sick with pneumonia and was even in the hospital for a week. I am just now recuperated enough to work again.

"But I'll be going there as soon as possible, early next week, if I can get a ticket. You call me back next week and I can tell you more. You just need to have patience. That's all. Everything will be okay."

So much for that, I thought.

Before he left, Lloyd, true to his promise, left a

small pair of binoculars. I crouched by the window and trained them on Nila's apartment. I watched off and on all day, but a curtain never stirred.

I felt very alone that long afternoon. Lloyd hadn't said when they'd be back. Maybe they'd gone to check on escape routes, or perhaps they were out posing as American businessmen. Their cover, Lloyd told me, was that they were in Bolivia to buy wedding dresses for export. This involved going to shops, talking to manufacturers, having conferences, discussing contracts, and whatever else went into it.

There was no TV or radio in the room to break the silence. The *soroche* made me unutterably fatigued and I slept again. I was awakened by the sound of explosives going off in the streets nearby. I knew from Lloyd that the current conflict had to do with tin miners protesting the freeze on their salaries, which was part of the government's attempt to stem the rampant inflation. The workers had come out of the tin mines in the country's interior and had swarmed the city by the thousands, marching in the streets and setting off sticks of dynamite. This time there was more urgency than usual on the part of the government to quell the unrest because of the Pope's impending visit.

Along with the miners, bus and taxi drivers were on strike, too. Most people depended on public transportation to get around, but in spite of the absence of buses and taxis, the streets were alive with people. They went about their daily business as best they could in spite of the turmoil surrounding them. I had never learned to handle the constant near-chaos with anything approaching the equanimity of the Bolivians. They took it as a matter of course.

As I sat watching the people outside, I felt as though I'd never left. I felt again the omnipresent frustration that had defined my life there. Throughout the afternoon memories kept bobbing to the surface of my mind. I remembered the impassive faces of the Indians in the open market as would-be buyers wrangled and pleaded for the food that they refused to sell because of the inflation. I remembered that buying milk for Jane and Michael hadn't meant a simple trip to the store—it was a daily quest. Finding a bag of flour to make bread with was a major coup. The fifty-pound bag would be zealously locked up at home (so the maid wouldn't pilfer it) and parceled out to one's relatives. Once when no meat was to be found in the city, we had piled into a Jeep with some of Federico's relatives and made a trek to the countryside, where we'd bought a pig from a peasant farmer, who'd slaughtered it for us on the spot.

Later that evening the men finally returned. Bob bounced in and asked merrily, "Did you hear the boom-booms?" I laughed. He could probably make jokes during a nuclear holocaust. His cheerful optimism was ballast to Lloyd's gloomy pronouncements and my own anxiety.

I told Lloyd about my phone call to Dr. Castillo and about the fact that he hadn't yet had my papers validated by the Supreme Court. Lloyd grunted, "Not good. Well, we'll just have to make sure we don't get caught."

He decided it was time for me to study the layout

162

of the children's school, Amor de Dios. We went down to the Jeep in relays, first Bob, then Guy, with Lloyd and me last, to prevent the hotel security men from knowing we were together. The school was only a few blocks away, down the street from the hotel and Nila's apartment building.

It was a handsome two-story building in the Spanish colonial style, with cream colored walls and arched doors and windows framed in dark, polished wood. It was surrounded by a tall wrought-iron fence. One building away on the other side of it was the residence of the President of Bolivia. Across from the Presidential Palace was the headquarters of the military police. MP's armed with automatic weapons roamed the street at all hours of the day and night. The street also happened to be part of Embassy Row — all along the sidewalk, sentry boxes with guards inside marked the entrances of several foreign embassies. Federico had chosen a well-guarded fortress in which to put the children.

For weeks Bob had been hanging around the school. He was there early every morning before the first bell rang. He would sit in the bus with the driver and make small talk, and nod to the nuns as they passed by. He would stroll up and down the sidewalk and chat with the school guard at the gate. Posing as a parent interested in enrolling his child, he had even met with the Mother Superior, the principal of the school, and obtained schedules and other valuable information. He could probably have found his way through the school's corridors blindfolded. In fact, he'd become such a familiar figure that nobody paid particular attention to him anymore. He was just a friendly, slightly eccentric gringo.

Now several cars were parked in front of the school, even though classes had been over for hours and dusk had fallen. "There's Federico's car," Bob said. He pointed to a gray Jeep parked among the others.

"Looks like they're having some kind of PTA meeting," Lloyd observed. I wondered if Federico would have brought Jane and Michael with him. What would it be like to see them now, from so close?

"Here they come," Lloyd muttered. I shrank farther into the backseat as several people emerged from the school. I recognized Federico as he moved into the glow of the streetlight. He was neatly dressed in a coat and tie, and his dark hair was gleaming.

"He always dresses impeccably," Lloyd mused, "which is strange, since he doesn't have a job, as near as we can tell. After taking the kids to school he just goes back home. Every once in a while he'll go downtown." I felt a rush of pity for him in spite of myself. Maybe the suit was a pathetic front to convince the world that he had important things to do. Maybe dressing well was his last remaining vestige of pride. Anyway, he certainly seemed confident now, even cocky, as he took center stage in the group of parents. He held forth about something, gesturing expansively as he talked, for about twenty minutes. He had always been so good at talking—smooth, convincing, polite. He liked nothing better than to have a captive audience while he lectured, and he was certainly in his element now. Finally the parents shook

164

hands all around, with kisses on the cheeks for the ladies, and then Federico got in his Jeep and drove away.

It was then that I recognized the apartment building next to the school. It was the same one where Food Aid International kept an apartment for volunteers. Russ had lived there until recently. Even though I'd been in the apartment several times, I'd never paid attention to the school next door. What an incredible coincidence!

"That's where the Food Aid International apartment is," I told Lloyd excitedly.

"What? That place?" He peered into the darkness at the boxy three-story building. "You're kidding! Damn, I wish we'd known that earlier. It would've been a perfect place to watch the children from."

I said nothing. I hadn't tried to contact Russ or anybody I knew from Food Aid International. For one thing, I didn't want him to get into any trouble on my account. He'd already stuck his neck out enough. And after all, he would still be here to take the heat long after I was gone. For another thing, I couldn't in good conscience do anything to jeopardize its missions. The Bolivian government would surely frown on a foreign organization meddling in the affairs of its citizens, not to mention flouting its laws.

Bob pulled the Jeep up opposite the sloping concrete walkway that ran alongside the school. It was about a hundred feet long and led to the schoolyard in back. A chain-link fence separated it from the apartment building next door. At sidewalk level a gate closed off the ramp.

Bob pointed toward the gate. "There's a guard there every morning, an old guy. He stands there while the kids go in and then he locks the gate after the last bell rings."

Lloyd said tersely, "We're talking about a thirty-second operation. You'll have that long to intercept the children, get past the guard, and get into the Jeep." He pointed down the walkway. "At the bottom of that ramp and around the corner is a bathroom. You'll hide in there while you're waiting for the children to arrive."

"How will I know when to come out?"

"We might use two-way radios. Or maybe some other signal."

The vagueness of the plan made me uneasy. I peered down the ramp to the murky darkness at the bottom. So this was where it was going to happen. All of a sudden it was becoming very real.

Back at the hotel, Lloyd gave me instructions for the next day. I was to call up Dr. Castillo and tell him that I had come to Bolivia thinking that the papers had been signed and I could go home with my children. After all, Dr. Castillo had told me it would take only two months. If I couldn't leave with my children, then I wanted at least to get their passports. I was to demand that he accompany me to the Consulate to help me get them.

"Tell him it's *vital* that you get the passports now. You don't want to wait around for months until it's

166

time to come get the children, and then have to wait around some more just for passports."

"What about my phone call with him today? He thinks I was calling from the States. Besides, he already told me today that the papers aren't signed yet. How am I supposed to explain that all of a sudden I'm here in La Paz and don't remember anything he said the day before?"

Without batting an eyelash, Lloyd replied, "You'll think of something."

Then he and Bob left. It was decided that Guy would sleep on one of the sofas in the sitting room next door. I was tired and went to bed early but tossed and turned all night.

Chapter Twelve

Friday, April 22, 1988

The three men went to Amor de Dios in the morning to watch Federico deliver Jane and Michael to school. Their report was bad. Federico had taken both children by the hand and walked them all the way down the ramp. Michael had struggled to break free but Federico had held on tight.

"We don't know what this means," Lloyd said, "but he's never done it before. Of course, if he keeps it up, it'll be impossible to get those children."

My throat went dry. "Maybe he knows I'm here."

"Maybe. Or maybe it's something that came out of that meeting last night at the school. What bothers me even more, though, is that there were *two* guards at the gate, not just one. We spotted two plainclothesmen outside the school, too."

"How did you know they were plainclothesmen?" I asked.

"When you've been in the business as long as I

have, you can tell," he said. "Anyway, we've got to move fast. The longer we're down here, the riskier it is."

I felt the tears welling up and blinked them back.

Lloyd noticed and warned, "You've been holding up well so far. You've got to continue to keep logic over emotions." He left me alone to call Dr. Castillo.

An icy band of fear squeezed my chest—fear that I might fail, fear for Jane and Michael should I fail. What then? What would the rest of their lives be like? Lloyd's words from the other night ricocheted around in my brain: *They never smile. They're like little robots.*

No, I scolded myself . . . don't get carried away by negative thoughts. Anticipating such moments of panic, I had scribbled some phrases in a small notebook that I carried in my purse. I took the notebook out now and thumbed through it.

"The Lord is my helper; I will not be afraid." *Hebrews 13:6.* This was a Bible verse that Jane had had to memorize for her first-grade class at St. Paul's Lutheran School in McAllen. During the long months since I'd last seen her, I'd kept it posted on my refrigerator.

"Fear not." *Jesus.* Then, a piece of wisdom from Mr. Rosenthal, who was always chiding me for worrying too much about events I had no control over: "Do all that you can, then don't worry about the results."

Next, from Martin Luther: "God is the being of

169

all that are and the life of all that live and the wisdom of all the wise, for all things have their being more truly in God than in themselves." Daddy had given me that one. For some reason, it comforted me, too.

As I read and reread the phrases, my thoughts and fears were quieted. I put the book away and called Dr. Castillo.

"Catereen? Where are you calling from?" He was understandably puzzled that I was calling back so soon.

"I'm here in La Paz," I replied. His voice registered surprise. "In La Paz? Aqui?"

This was not going to be easy.

I told him that I had been in La Paz when I'd called the day before, but that I'd had a bad case of *soroche*.

"To tell the truth, I don't remember a thing we talked about yesterday."

To my utter amazement he bought it. Even better, he agreed without hesitation to meet with me that very morning and accompany me to get the passports. I hung up and gave Lloyd and the men the good news. Then I set about getting ready. I was excited at the prospect of getting out of the hotel room, where I was beginning to feel like a prisoner in solitary confinement. It was also a relief to take off the wig and shake out my real hair. I tried to fluff some life into the lanky strands. In the middle of my swipes with the brush, I stopped and gave myself a wry smile in the mirror. At a time like this,

170

what did it matter what I looked like? Oh, well, old habits were hard to break. Susan used to tease me that I couldn't go outside to throw out the trash without having my makeup on.

I changed from my jeans into a pair of black slacks and put my gray corduroy blazer over my sweater. In a few minutes I was ready.

Again we went down to the Jeep in relays. This time, Guy went to the lobby first to watch for anyone who might be paying particular attention to us. The men were aware that they'd been under surveillance since their arrival in La Paz. Then Bob went down in the elevator, followed by me and then Lloyd. I felt quite exposed without my wig. Once in the Jeep, I slouched low in the backseat as we drove along the back streets toward downtown.

"Man, I've never seen a hotel crawling with so many security people!" Bob said.

"Really? Where?" I hadn't noticed any.

"They're all over that place. When I was checking you into the hotel on Wednesday night, twice one of 'em tried to make off with your suitcase. He said he would help me with my luggage, and I kept tellin' him I didn't *want* his help. One night," Bob chuckled, "I was standin' outside the hotel nightclub—listening to some guy singing and playing the guitar. I heard something behind me and *damn* if it wasn't a security guard with a two-way radio. He was sayin' "—here Bob imitated the self-important tones of the guard—'The gringo is standing *outside* the nightclub, listening to the entertainer.' " Bob

171

laughed, "I guess they were mad 'cuz I didn't pay to go in."

Bob shifted the Jeep into first gear and it labored up a steep downtown street. The city was laid out so that the main street wound through the town at its lowest point, at the bottom of the huge crevice where La Paz lay. The streets intersecting the main road went straight up the canyon walls. I'd always hated to drive there, and had preferred even the discomfort of a crowded taxi or bus. The trickiest part was stopping and starting halfway up a hill without plowing into the car in front of you or sliding into the car behind. A standard transmission was almost a necessity.

Dr. Castillo was waiting outside the building, as promised. His sonorous voice belied his thin, bespectacled appearance. Thick glasses perched on a large nose, under which a moustache bristled. His ears were huge and his earlobes were like flaps. He greeted me warmly and then led me up three flights of concrete stairs. I still wasn't used to the lack of oxygen at this altitude, and by the time we reached his office on the third floor I was out of breath.

By American standards his office was shabby and ill-equipped, in a time warp—reminiscent of the fifties, or even the forties. In the anteroom, a wooden desk held a manual typewriter and a pile of carbon paper. A sofa, scattered wooden chairs, and a battered coffee table piled with magazines completed the furnishings. Above the desk in Dr. Castillo's inner office hung a calendar of naked women—standard office equipment in Bolivia.

We sat down and Dr. Castillo first went over my file with me, explaining in detail what each document was. There was nothing in it that I didn't already know about from my previous conversations with him.

Then we walked to the nearby courthouse, a dreary, ancient building with high ceilings and chipped plaster. Dr. Castillo reminded me that he had once been a judge before the fickle winds of political change had swept him out. The judge in charge of my case was an old friend of his. But the encouragement I felt upon hearing that piece of news evaporated as soon as I saw Don Carlitos. He was a tiny old man with bleary eyes who seemed to be only tenuously aware of his surroundings. He peered up at me dimly as Dr. Castillo introduced us. Then Dr. Castillo talked about the case while I watched Don Carlitos shakily light a filter cigarette at the wrong end. He then calmly broke off the tip of the cigarette and relit it at the correct end.

After listening to Dr. Castillo recap the situation, Don Carlitos assured us that as soon as the papers were signed by the Supreme Court, Federico's suit for custody would be annulled. But, he added ominously, Federico had the right to appeal, and the outcome of that appeal was *otra cosa,* another thing. Dr. Castillo thanked Don Carlitos profusely for his time and we shook hands all around. I got the distinct feeling that Don Carlitos had already forgotten who I was.

173

Now I was confused. It seemed that things were not as simple as Dr. Castillo had led me to believe. What was the appeal that Don Carlitos had mentioned? How did that work? Dr. Castillo explained as we walked the few blocks to the consulate. Federico had the right to appeal the decision if the Supreme Court annulled his lawsuit. How long would the appeal take? It depended on how hard Federico fought. He could keep bringing up new arguments and prolong it indefinitely. Then suddenly and without preamble, Dr. Castillo announced, "The best thing would be just to snatch them back yourself."

I couldn't believe my ears. "You mean, kidnap them back?"

"Yes," he said simply. "I have a friend, a *capitan,* who is the assistant to the Minister of the Interior. I think he could help you." The Minister of the Interior was probably the most feared person in the Bolivian Government, and, next to the President, the most powerful. He was responsible for arresting political prisoners, who were then thrown in cells somewhere in the ministry building. There they were held without benefit of trial. Sometimes they were tortured. It had even happened to American journalists. The minister's assistant would be in a position of considerable power, too. Getting the kids out of Bolivia would be child's play with him on our side. But if he couldn't be trusted, we'd all be put at considerable risk.

I played dumb. "Do you really think I could get

away with such a thing?"

"I am sure that you could. But you would need assistance. The *capitan* could be very helpful. The least he could do would be to get exit papers for the children to cross the border with." Anyone who wanted to leave Bolivia with minors had to get a government permit to do so. Getting permits was a wearisome process that I was all too familiar with. It required half a dozen photos of each child, the physical presence of both parents and children at the government ministry that issued permits for minors to travel with their parents, and a blizzard of signatures and stamps. Both parents had to give their permission in writing and in person for a child to travel with the other parent. These permits had to be produced at airports before boarding, even for in-country flights, and at all border crossings.

The system was designed to prevent child kidnappings. In Bolivia I was always hearing horror stories about children being snatched by strangers and sold abroad to adoption rings. A more common occurrence, however, was that the kidnapped children, nearly always Indians, were sold into virtual slavery *within* Bolivia. Indian merchants would use the children as pack animals for hauling merchandise in the markets and for doing chores around the house. Sometimes the parents themselves would sell one of their children. At least that way, they knew the child would have food and shelter.

At any rate, it would be a great help to get my hands on legal exit permits for Jane and Michael.

By then we'd arrived at the consulate. Dr. Castillo whispered that we'd discuss El Capitan later.

The Consulate was on the third floor of an edifice that was indistinguishable from the other old buildings on the street. Inside, a Marine guard directed us through a security arch before allowing us to enter. The woman at the counter greeted Dr. Castillo by name. In a few moments a tall man with thinning red hair came out and extended his hand.

"I'm Steven Dunlop. I'm very glad to meet you, Mrs. Bascope," he said warmly. I recognized his name from my conversations with Dr. Castillo. Steven Dunlop was the Vice Consul in La Paz. He seemed to know who I was, too, and ushered us into his office. Within moments we were joined by a Bolivian man and woman. I was pleasantly surprised at our reception. They all seemed to have dropped whatever they were doing for our unannounced visit.

Dunlop began by making introductions. Dr. Garza was the attorney for the U.S. Embassy. Alicia had been the representative from the consulate who had made the last welfare and whereabouts visit to see Jane and Michael. She leaned over and touched my arm.

"Your children are beautiful," she said.

"Thank you," I said and struggled to keep back sudden tears. "Are they all right?"

"Yes, they seemed well cared for and happy." She added hastily, "I'm sure they miss you very much, though."

I explained my sudden appearance in Bolivia with the same story I had told Dr. Castillo: I thought everything had been taken care of and I could simply come down and pick up Jane and Michael. Now that Dr. Castillo had explained the impossibility of that, at least for now, I would like to get passports for the children. And to see them. Dr. Garza shook his head.

"I'm afraid that it's impossible for you to see your children. In fact, you are in a very precarious situation. If your husband finds out you are here and serves you with legal papers, you would be forced to remain in Bolivia for the duration of the lawsuit. And that could take a long time."

"Where are you staying now?" Dunlop asked.

I thought quickly. Lloyd had told me not to tell anyone about him or Bob or Guy. But I'd already told Dr. Castillo that I was staying at the Sheraton, so I couldn't very well make up something else now. "I'm at the Sheraton."

"You could easily be traced through your hotel registration and served with papers. Do you have any friends you could stay with?" Dunlop asked.

"I don't know," I said hesitantly.

Dr. Garza suggested. "You should at least change hotels, then. The first place they'd look would be the Sheraton, where all the gringos go. You could stay in a cheaper hotel, like the Libertador, down the street from here."

They all agreed that's what I should do. Then there ensued an hour-long discussion of the legal aspects of the situation and what my chances were of getting custody of Jane and Michael through the Bolivian court system. The embassy lawyer agreed with Dr. Castillo's assessment that I would almost surely be awarded custody of the children—*eventually*. But Federico had already been granted temporary custody. Worse, his petition was full of damning accusations, about drug use, consorting with drug dealers, sleeping around.

"It's obvious that Sr. Bascope is after revenge," said Dr. Castillo.

"Yes," Dr. Garza agreed with a tone of disgust, as he leafed through a copy of Federico's custody petition. "This has nothing to do with what's best for the children." He laid aside the petition. "The things he is claiming are very bad, very damaging. But," he said, "if they are untrue, then there is no evidence, no proof. And without proof . . ." he waved his hand in a gesture of dismissal, "you would be awarded the children." Then he echoed Don Carlitos' words. "But of course he would still have the right of appeal."

Dunlop, who had been in Bolivia only a few weeks and hadn't mastered Spanish yet, had been struggling to follow the conversation. I gave him a summary in English.

"So," Dunlop asked, "if the Supreme Court annuls Mr. Bascope's case, how long would the appeal take?"

"It depends," said Dr. Garza. "If Sr. Bascope doesn't put up a fight, it could be over soon. If he fights—and I believe he will—it could take a year, maybe longer." He turned to me. "But in the end, you would get the children."

Steven Dunlop shifted uncomfortably in his chair. "I'm not so sure. I've never seen things happen that easily. There's always a factor of doubt."

Dr. Garza spoke up. "Of course, the political factor enters into it, too."

There was a long pause. We all knew that the political factor would change everything. Dr. Garza finally broke the silence.

"Your best bet," he said, "is simply to snatch them back and make a run for it."

"My sentiments exactly," Dr. Castillo said firmly.

For the second time that day, I couldn't believe what I was hearing. Could it be that these two attorneys, Dr. Castillo and Dr. Garza, were advocating that I violate the laws of their country? I glanced at Dunlop. He nodded, "I think they're right."

I stammered, "I thought the embassy couldn't be involved in anything like that."

"Knowing about it and being involved in it are two different things," Dunlop replied. "We can't help you get possession of the children or leave the country with them. But they are legally entitled to passports. We can try to get those for you."

I fixed what I hoped was a disingenuous gaze on my face as I listened to them offer advice on how to resnatch the children, what routes to use to take them out of the country, what documents I would need. Of course, by now I knew more than they did about it.

"Copacabana or Desaguadero would probably be the best places to cross the border," Dr. Garza was saying. "Stay away from the airport. You'll need exit visas, of course. I don't know how you're going to get those."

"I know someone who could get those for her," Dr. Castillo offered. El Capitan to the rescue.

"At the border you could tell them you're a tourist and didn't know about the exit visas," said Dunlop. "If you offered money, you might get away with that."

"What about entry visas? The kids' passports wouldn't show that they ever entered Bolivia. Won't they question that?" I asked.

"Tell them you lost their passports while you were here and they were just reissued," said Dr. Garza.

"What about the passports?" I asked. "Is it possible for me to get them today?"

"Today? No, that's not possible," Dunlop said. "Normally it takes five working days to process them. They have to be approved by the State Department in Washington first, and here we don't have a telex as other consulates do in the bigger capitals. What we do is send the applications to Lima and they telex them to Washington from there."

Five days! And what if the State Department in Washington blew the whistle on me? I would just have to hope that the bureaucracy's right hand

180

wouldn't know what its left hand was doing.

Dunlop added, "I'll see what I can do. I'll try to have them for you on Monday."

It was twelve noon. Alicia glanced at her watch and everyone stood up. Lunchtime. Everything closed during the two-hour lunch period, and most people went home. We shook hands all around, and Dunlop escorted us to the door. He waited as Dr. Castillo walked ahead a few steps, then whispered, "Think it over carefully before you decide to do anything. There are risks involved. The problem is to know whom to trust." His forehead was creased with concern. I told him I would.

My spirits were soaring. They had been so kind, so full of concern and advice. I didn't feel nearly as alone as before, cooped up in the hotel with only my anxious thoughts to keep me company. Monday I would have the passports. Soon I could be leaving here with my children. My outlook was brighter than it had been since I'd arrived. Had it been only two days ago? It seemed much longer.

Dr. Castillo and I decided to discuss more about El Capitan over lunch. In the tiny upstairs restaurant there was barely enough room to squeeze between the tables. The restaurant was already full, and we were seated at a table with an elderly German woman. During our meal, she mumbled continuously to herself and slipped food from her plate into her purse. There was no menu—only the special for the day. First we were served the appetizer: a slice of bread decorated with swirls of mustard and ketchup. I set mine aside to wait for the next course, homemade peanut soup.

In such close quarters it was impossible to discuss kidnapping plans, so the conversation took a more personal turn.

Dr. Castillo told me a little about his own divorce and how it had affected his relationship with his only child, a son.

I leaned across the table toward him. "I wish there were some way that Federico and I could reach a compromise, before I make any plans to try to kidnap them back. I never wanted it to be this way. I don't want them to be without a father."

"I could try to talk to his lawyer about it," Dr. Castillo offered. "His name is Ruben Aguilar. I know him."

"If he would let the kids come back and live with me, I'd send them to Bolivia every year to spend the summers with him. Of course I'd need some kind of guarantee that he'd let me have them back. Wouldn't it be great if he'd agree to something like that?"

Indeed it would. Then I could cancel the whole risky kidnap operation, the kids could have both Mommy and Daddy, Mommy and Daddy could both have the kids, and everyone would live happily ever after. Maybe too much to hope for, but it could happen.

Dr. Castillo said, "Catereen, I don't know you well. But I can tell that you're not a bad person. You didn't deserve this. You will get your children back."

I felt I could trust Dr. Castillo, that he really did have my best interests at heart.

Before we parted, he said he would try to get in touch with El Capitan the following morning. I would call him Saturday afternoon to learn the outcome of their conversation.

Back at the hotel, I gave my report to the men. They were encouraged by the news that the passports would be ready by Monday and as surprised as I was that the people at the consulate had been so helpful.

"You didn't mention us, did you?" Lloyd asked sharply.

"No, of course not. Dr. Castillo doesn't know anything either." Lloyd was especially interested in El Capitan and what he could do for us. He and Bob started arguing about whether to bring El Capitan in on the plans.

Lloyd said, "I think we ought to hear his ideas. We might find out something useful."

Bob's blue eyes were uncharacteristically icy. "Lloyd, I've seen it happen time and time again: each person you bring in decreases your chances of success by 25%. It's just too risky. How do we know we can trust this guy? What do we know about him?" His voice rose in exasperation. "Hell, we don't even know his name!"

Guy sat there quietly listening. Apparently he was used to scenes like these. He caught my eye and made a face as Lloyd and Bob wrangled back and forth. It was to become a familiar occurrence over the next few days.

But Lloyd was the boss, and he had the final word: if El Capitan offered to help, I was to listen to his ideas and then pass them on to Lloyd. Lloyd also decided that it would be best for me to get out of the hotel and stay somewhere else—like at the Food Aid International apartment. There I would be safe from discovery and I could keep a watch on the children's comings and goings at the school. I was hesitant about bringing FAI into it, but then I supposed there would be no harm in simply staying in the apartment.

When I called the office, I was told that Russ was in Tahiti on his honeymoon. Good . . . that meant he wouldn't be implicated in any of this. I talked to Roberto, the Bolivian who was in charge in Russ's absence. We knew each other from when I'd worked there. As soon as I told Roberto that I was in La Paz, he offered me a place to stay—in Russ's old apartment. I didn't even have to ask.

"There are two couples living there now," he explained, "but there's plenty of room for you too. Anyway, Ben and Susana will be out in the countryside for the next few days."

Roberto offered to pick me up from the hotel and drive me to the apartment. I told Lloyd, Bob, and Guy the good news and then quickly gathered together my things and met Roberto outside. On the way to the apartment, I told him my by now well-rehearsed cover story and he caught me up on FAI

184

news. Russ had just gotten married to a Bolivian woman. Ben, a Hunger Corps volunteer from the States, had recently gotten married to a Bolivian girl, too. She worked with him in the village of Tairo by Lake Titicaca, where they lived alongside the Indians in a mud hut with no electricity and no plumbing. When they were in town, they lived in the FAI apartment.

The other couple staying at the apartment was new to Bolivia, having just arrived from the Midwest about two weeks ago. They were still in training, learning the language and visiting different FAI projects. I looked forward eagerly to meeting them. By now I was desperate for human company. Sure, there were Lloyd, Bob, and Guy. They made certain that I had everything I needed physically. But they were usually gone, or locked into the room next to mine. And I was forbidden to call anyone back home. I knew that the volunteers in the FAI apartment would be kind, concerned, and caring, and I was ready to soak it all up like a sponge.

We drove past Amor de Dios. The gate was closed and the windows were dark. Roberto drove to the small parking lot in the rear of the apartment building. We walked up three flights of outside stairs and then down a corridor to the FAI apartment in the corner. Dan and Jennifer answered the doorbell. They were young, probably in their early twenties. Dan was stocky and blond, with a brash all-American grin. Jennifer, her pale face framed by a cloud of dark hair, seemed more serious and quiet.

They showed me to my room: a maid's cubicle about four feet by six feet, with a single cot squeezed into it. Behind it was the *lavanderia,* a dank room with a cement sink for washing clothes. Its ceiling was festooned with clotheslines hung with an assortment of dripping pants, underwear, and shirts.

Dan and Jennifer assured me that I was welcome to stay as long as I needed to. They showed me where to find extra blankets in the hall closet. A few minutes later, they had to leave for a dinner invitation.

I explored the apartment. It was just as I had remembered it when, three years earlier, my friend and coworker at FAI, Gloria, had lived there. Gloria was a bubbly Texan from Houston, and like me, had married a Bolivian and moved to Bolivia. They had gotten a divorce shortly before she'd begun working at FAI. It was Gloria who had "discovered" this apartment. I smiled to myself. Count on Gloria, who loved her creature comforts, to find the coziest apartment this side of the Chuquiyapu River.

By American standards it was lacking in several departments—the toilet flushed at whim, the "shower" was more of a trickle, the hot water was gone in minutes, and there was no heat. But by Bolivian standards it was luxurious indeed. For one thing, it boasted wall-to-wall carpeting instead of the usual wooden floors. But its most attractive features were the two solid walls of south windows in the living room, where the sun shining through phPsignificantly raised the temperature of the r   o   o   m In the afternoon you could strip down to shirt-sleeves and bask in the sun like a cat.

But what was most important to me now was the perfect view the windows afforded of the children's school. The coincidence was almost uncanny. I considered it an encouraging sign. Perhaps God was smiling on this venture after all.

I fixed myself a plain supper of rice, bread, and hot chocolate. Then I sat on the sofa next to the living room window. It was already dark, but for a long time I gazed out at the schoolyard and tried to imagine Jane and Michael running and playing there every day.

I was in bed before Dan and Jennifer returned. The night was chilly, and it didn't help that the tiny windows high up on the walls of the room wouldn't close. A bare light bulb from the corridor outside shined into my eyes. I burrowed deeper into the sleeping bag—which smelled as if it had held many an unwashed volunteer just in from the country-side—and tried to sleep.

Chapter Thirteen

Saturday, April 23, 1988

I woke up aching all over and sniffling. Great, I thought. Added to the altitude sickness and a still painful sunburn, I now had a miserable cold.

Dan and Jennifer left early to go to El Alto, the slum area on the *altiplano* surrounding La Paz, to look over some of the FAI feeding centers. I showered, teeth chattering, in a thin trickle of lukewarm water. Then I gratefully washed out some clothes. I had packed light, expecting to be in Bolivia only two or three days, and by now I had worn everything several times without a washing. Clean clothes would feel good. My blue jeans would have to remain unwashed—it would take days for them to drip dry in the laundry room and I would surely need them before then.

Early in the afternoon, I called Dr. Castillo. His meeting with Federico's lawyer had not been fruitful. Ruben Aguilar had flatly refused to consider any sort of compromise. Dr. Castillo was a little disquieted by some of the things Federico had told his lawyer about me. As he reeled them off, I laughed out loud at Federico's creativity, which seemed to increase with time. One of his new allegations was that my first lawyer had quit working for me and had sought out Federico to represent him instead. I assured Dr. Castillo that none of it was true.

With relief in his voice he said, "Then you have nothing to worry about." He added that he hadn't been able to get in touch with El Capitan, but would keep trying.

I wandered into the living room to enjoy the sun streaming in the windows. The view to the east was breathtaking. Just behind the parking lot, there was a sheer drop into a valley below. Cars snaked along a road that had been chiseled into the red cliffs of the canyon, and even through the windowpanes I could hear the roar of the Chuquiyapu River below.

The road led into the bedroom suburbs of La Paz, where Embassy personnel lived in huge houses surrounded by well-manicured gardens. We had rented a house in a more modest middle-class section of one of those suburbs. There were many, but I couldn't remember their names anymore, not even the subdivision where we'd bought a piece of land, planning to build a house someday. After a while I turned away from the window.

I spent the afternoon laboriously composing a

letter in Spanish to the Mother Superior at Amor de Dios. Lloyd thought that in a pinch such a letter might come in handy. It might at least buy some time if we presented it when we tried to take the children. I rather doubted that the Mother Superior would take the time to read a 15-page letter while two of her charges were being spirited away. But better to leave no stone unturned. At least the letter spelled out that I had legal custody of the children as far as the United States was concerned, and that Federico had taken them illegally. As proof we would enclose translated copies of the Texas court documents.

When Dan and Jennifer got back that night, they made a delicious supper of rice and fresh baked fish. Roberto had already told Dan and Jennifer my basic cover story. I was relieved that they hadn't asked a lot of questions up to now. But tonight the inevitable question came out: "Why don't you just kidnap them back?" I looked into their eyes and was about to tell them the usual lie, that first I wanted to go the legal route. Instead I hesitated, then admitted, "Well, I've been considering that."

Immediately Dan was bursting with ideas on how it could be carried out. He ended up outlining a plan almost identical to Lloyd's—which wasn't surprising, considering how few options there were. But Dan added a new wrinkle: Jennifer, posing as a schoolgirl, could help. Like all the other children in the Amor de Dios, she could wear a white duster over her clothes. Her Mona Lisa coloring and delicate features made her indistinguishable from the older girls at the school. Most of them were from upper-class Bolivian families, descendants of the Spaniards who did not have the dark skin and coarser features of the native Indians.

"Jennifer can stop the kids as they're coming down the ramp. Nobody would think anything about her taking them back out the gate to buy candy or something." Candy vendors set up their stands just outside the school gate every morning. "You could be waiting by the candy stand and just take them from there. I could be a lookout, or maybe even distract the guard or the MP's who are out there directing traffic in front of the school. I could be the dumb gringo tourist asking directions or something. And Jennifer could slip in and out so fast that nobody would notice her."

Jennifer sat quietly listening to all this. She added, "In fact, Dan could be on the other side of the fence, in our driveway. You could be there with him, where the kids could see you. You could talk to them through the fence and they'd go back up the ramp with me for sure."

But would they? I wondered. This was one of my deepest fears about the whole operation. What if Federico had brainwashed the kids to be afraid of me? What if they refused to go with me?

Surely Federico had coached them for the possibility that I might show up someday. Surely he wouldn't risk making the same mistake I had.

Mr. Rosenthal had scoffed at my worries: "Cass, they'll go with you. The minute they see you they're gonna forget anything he might have said. I don't doubt that in the slightest."

But it still ate at me. After all, everything depended on it.

Inevitably, after holding it in so long and with the relief of having a sympathetic audience, I confided in Dan and Jennifer. I told them I had come to Bolivia to resnatch Jane and Michael. I also told them about Lloyd, Bob, and Guy, although I didn't give any names — and then swore them to secrecy. Dan and Jennifer were more eager than ever to help.

"I can just imagine what the folks back home will say when we tell them we helped kidnap two kids out of Bolivia!" Dan crowed.

I cautioned, "Be sure you really want to do this. Think it over before you decide. I don't want anybody to get in trouble." They said there was no thinking to do; their decision was made.

Their enthusiasm was catching. Already I felt more confident about our prospects. With Dan and Jennifer playing their roles, the plan was so much more workable — there were fewer things to go wrong, fewer things to arouse suspicion. If I were the one trying to go down the ramp, the guard might stop me. Or I might be discovered as I was hiding in the bathroom. Riskiest of all, I might be stopped while trying to leave with the kids. Let's face it, in a country of short dark people, a tall blonde stuck out. I wouldn't have the security of the wig to hide behind. It might scare or confuse Jane and Michael. And maybe Federico had alerted the people at the school to watch for me.

Yes, the plan *could* work with Dan and Jennifer.

Lloyd called the next day, using the prearranged code: two rings, a pause, two rings, a pause, and then on the third set of rings I'd answer. He came by the apartment after Dan and Jennifer left for church. Striding to the living room windows he exulted, "This is amazing! The location is perfect!" He turned to me, his face glowing. "In fact, it's more than that—it's downright providential! I almost feel like I'm on a divine mission." I hadn't ever seen him so enthusiastic.

"We finally got a room at the Crillon. You know, we tried to before, but it was full." The Crillon was an old hotel next door to Nila's apartment building. Now Lloyd and the men would be able to monitor Federico's comings and goings, with or without the children, from their hotel room.

"I feel really confident about the whole operation," he said, echoing my thoughts. He perched his bulk gingerly on the edge of a small bench and leaned forward earnestly. "I feel more confident about your part in this too. At first, I have to admit I was skeptical about you. I thought you were too emotionally involved to be effective. But since we've been here in Bolivia, I've gotten to know you better. I've seen that you have courage and insight and intelligence. I respect your ideas. And you're a lot tougher than you look." He smiled, "In fact, I consider you part of the team now." I wondered if that meant I'd be told what was going on from now on. Nevertheless I was pleased with his unexpected praise.

I told Lloyd about Dan's and Jennifer's offer to help. To my surprise he seized on the idea. He said that he had already considered getting a Bolivian to play the schoolgirl role. He would talk over the plans with Dan and Jennifer after I got the passports on Monday. In the meantime, Lloyd gave me another assignment. After he left, I spent the rest of the morning drawing a detailed map of the school and schoolyard.

Just over the chain-link fence separating the apartment building from the school was the ramp sloping down from the front gate into the schoolyard. At the bottom of the ramp twelve steps led at right angles into the basketball/soccer court. Just around the corner of the ramp was a girls' bathroom. Large windows from the classrooms on both floors overlooked the schoolyard. If you kept going straight instead of going to the right at the bottom of the ramp, there were four steps leading up into a smaller courtyard raised some six feet above the basketball court. A storage shed stood against the fence that separated that court from the driveway of the apartment building. I drew the map to scale as best I could, and then carefully labeled everything.

After lunch I lay down to rest. The lack of oxygen combined with my cold made me tire easily, and I slept. Sometime later I was awakened by the sounds of a Bolivian brass band. I went to the window and looked out. The school was having some kind of fiesta. Crepe-paper streamers were strung across the basketball court, and children and adults milled around refreshment stands. Quickly I scanned the crowd for Jane and Michael. They weren't there.

I sat idly watching the scene for a while, wondering about the occasion for the festivities. Then a familiar movement on the far side of the court caught my eye: a little boy and girl hugged each other, then the girl impatiently wriggled free. In a convulsive motion my fingers dug into the back of the sofa.

"My babies!" I cried out. My beautiful children! Jane looked proper and ladylike in a long, dark dress and white stockings. Her long hair was cropped shorter, and it was pulled back severely from her face. Michael seemed paler and a little taller. I spotted Federico behind them, helping out in one of the stands.

I watched them all afternoon, studying them for clues as to how they *really* were. Jane seemed more subdued, while Michael was wilder, uncontrolled. They didn't mingle with the other kids and never strayed more than a few feet from Federico. With mixed feelings I watched him take them by the hand, smile down at them, buy them sodas. At least he was not the cold monster Lloyd and Bob had described. He was kind to them. They were loved. It was comforting to know that. Yet they seemed different somehow — as if they had lost some indefinable spark of childish joy.

At one point they sat almost directly under my window. I could have called their names and they would have looked up and seen me. How I ached to run down and touch their hands through the fence! As it was, all I could do was to look down at the tops of their heads and weep helplessly. I had to wait for just the right moment. There was no room for mistakes. I would have only this one chance.

Chapter Fourteen

Monday, April 25, 1988

The next morning at 8:15 I was stationed in the living room watching the school through the curtains, timing how long it took to walk up and down the ramp. Lloyd wanted me to clock it for both adults and children, and to note whether they were going at a normal pace or quickly. It took an adult about 45 seconds to walk up the ramp and 30 or 35 seconds to go down. If he or she was walking quickly, it took 35 and 25 seconds, respectively. A child took a few seconds longer. Lloyd had said this was a 30 second operation. We'd be cutting it close.

As the time neared for the morning bell to ring, the stream of children coming down the ramp thinned to a trickle. I still hadn't seen Jane or Michael. Then, just as the bell rang, they came trotting down the ramp, rounded the corner into the courtyard, and took their places in line. They looked so small and vulnerable in their little white uniforms. There were ten or twelve ragged lines of children, ranging from the smallest, the preschool class that Michael was in, on up to the high school kids. Jane stood alone at the end of her line. One little girl approached her and took her hand, but then quickly left to resume her place as the teachers began a kind of inspection, walking up and down the rows straightening the lines. Michael was having a shoving match with another little boy, and a nun jerked him smartly into line. Then the teachers took their place at the heads of the lines and led in the singing of the national anthem, followed by the school song. A whistle shrilled and they began filing into the building. Michael swung his lunchpail at the boy in front of him, stumbled, and fell. Then he jumped back to his feet. I smiled, but there was a huge lump in my throat. I watched until the last child disappeared inside.

I called the consulate to check on the children's passports and found out that they would not be ready until 4 P.M. that afternoon. I began wandering aimlessly through the apartment, wondering what to do for the rest of the day. Dan and Jennifer were at the FAI office, and I was alone again with time on my hands. I browsed through the bookshelf in the living room and read portions of travel books, mainly about the areas of Bolivia and Peru that we'd most likely go through if we went overland. I tried to memorize information:

the names of towns in Peru with flights to Lima, where to buy tickets for the railroad. Of course, Lloyd should already know all this stuff, I thought. Still, it didn't hurt to be prepared.

I took a nap after lunch. I still had a cold, but even in the best of health, I became fatigued quickly in La Paz because of the thin air. By now my sunburn had progressed to the stage where it wasn't painful anymore, just ugly. I looked like some kind of shedding reptile. My skin was peeling on every surface that had been exposed that day in Miami—in other words, over most of my body. I was glad the climate here made it necessary to keep my legs and arms covered up at all times.

Lloyd, Bob, and Guy arrived around 3:30. They were driving yet another rented Jeep—they changed vehicles every few days. Bob was wearing a wide-brimmed alpaca hat, the kind that tourists bought as souvenirs. As we drove up the steep street to the consulate, he tipped the hat cheerily to amused passersby. So much for keeping a low profile, I thought. Oh, well, that was how Bob operated. He had told me once that he had sprung people from prisons in Chile and Peru. How had he done it? Not from burrowing through secret tunnels or smuggling in metal files—but by noisily and conspicuously visiting the prisoner until the guards quit paying attention to him. Then he could do whatever needed to be done without being watched. He was using the same strategy now at the kids' school.

Bob parked outside the consulate to wait for me. Inside, Alicia greeted me and told me she would bring the passports out in a few minutes. As I waited I studied the travel advisories posted on the bulletin board. Ominously, most of the warnings had to do with travel in Peru. I took out my little notebook and carefully noted the names of areas to avoid. It seemed that the main dangers were road bandits and, even worse, sporadic violence by the terrorist group Sendero Luminoso ("Shining Path"), which was active in southern Peru, and in the province of Arequipa in particular.

Finally the passports were ready. Steven Dunlop came out to tell me good-bye.

"Have you decided what you're going to do yet?" he asked, clear eyes searching mine.

"No," I hedged, "not yet. But I think I might go for it."

He nodded and began to scribble something on a piece of paper. "If you get in trouble, call. Here's my office number, and this is my home phone." He took my hand in both his hands and squeezed it. "Good luck."

"Thank you." I was touched by his kindness.

Bob then drove me to Dr. Castillo's office.

"Catereen," he began in that regretful tone of voice I'd come to know well. "Mi amigo El

Capitan is in Cuba! He had to accompany the Minister of Interior there and he won't be back for a few days. I myself will be leaving for Sucre tomorrow, to get your papers signed." He beamed across his desk at me.

"Good," I said. Good that he'd be out of the way when I made my move. No sense in him being implicated.

"Go ahead and take your children back, Catereen," he encouraged me. "You can do it without the assistance of El Capitan. And don't worry about your lawsuit for custody. I'll continue with that even if you're successful in getting your children back."

"Maybe I will try, then."

He nodded, smiling. Then he asked me for a couple of favors: could I send him cassette tapes that taught English, and some price lists on Mace-type self-protection sprays, which he was interested in importing and selling in La Paz? I said I would. Before parting we gave each other the traditional parting hug, the *abrazo*.

By the time I got back to the apartment, Dan and Jennifer had arrived. I told them that Lloyd wanted to talk with them. They almost jumped up and down with excitement.

When Lloyd arrived later in the evening, he brought with him a school uniform and Jennifer tried it on. She looked perfect for the part of the schoolgirl.

201

Then Lloyd went over the plan. Dan would wait by the fence. I would be across the driveway from him, just inside the parking garage. Bob would stroll up and down the sidewalk in front of the school, as he did every day. He'd signal the arrival of Federico's Jeep by putting on his alpaca hat. Dan in turn would signal to Jennifer. This round-about procedure was necessary since neither Dan nor Jennifer had ever seen Federico or the kids, except from photographs, and they might not recognize them right away. Jennifer, dressed in the school uniform, was to go down the ramp just ahead of Jane and Michael. Then, as soon as Federico turned his back, she would take Jane and Michael by the hand and tell them that I was there. At that point I'd go to the fence and say something to them. Jennifer would lead them back up the ramp and out the gate and I would simply take their hands and walk to the getaway car. If Federico walked down the ramp with the children, then the plan would be aborted and we'd try again the next day.

After Lloyd left, Dan, Jennifer, and I were too excited to sleep. We were like high school kids before the big game. We stayed up playing cards and going over and over the plans. Around midnight, Bob came by to get the one small bag I'd be taking with me should we be successful. I would leave the rest of my clothes behind, along with my suitcase.

That night I slept fitfully. After all these months of waiting and planning, it was really about to happen.

We were up the following morning by six o'clock. Dan and Jennifer were too nervous to eat breakfast. I forced down a piece of bread to calm my fluttery stomach. I knew it might be a long time before my next meal.

We paced up and down the living room, waiting for the phone call telling us that Federico and the children were on their way. Lloyd would be watching for him from his room at the Crillon. At about 8:15 the phone rang and we all jumped.

A moment later we were trotting down the three flights of outside stairs. Then we took up our positions. Dan leaned casually against the fence. With his backpack and camera he looked like a tourist waiting for a ride. Jennifer, wearing her white duster, continued up the driveway and dawdled, tying her shoe, at the top of the driveway. I slid out of sight in the shadows of the parking garage. About 40 seconds went by. My heart pounded, then stood still—Federico and the children came into view not thirty feet in front of me. He was walking them down the ramp. I flattened myself against the wall of the garage. If Federico had been looking in my direction, he would have seen me. Today's attempt would have to be aborted.

After a few moments Jennifer joined Dan and me and we trudged back up the stairs to the apartment. The gardener eyed us curiously as we passed.

In a few minutes Bob rapped on the door. He rubbed his hands together and grinned, "That was only a dry run. Tomorrow we'll do it!" But Dan and Jennifer were a bit shaken. Dan thought someone across the street had been watching him through a window. We had aroused the suspicion of the gardener. But I felt calm, even confident. If Federico hadn't walked the kids down, it would have worked.

A rather subdued Dan and Jennifer left for work, and Lloyd, Guy, and Bob came over. Over dry bread and thick coffee, we discussed the morning's events, or rather, the lack of them. Lloyd agreed that it would have worked had circumstances been different. "In fact, it's the only plan with any *hope* of working," he said. "We'll try again tomorrow."

Later in the afternoon, a band was playing again at the school. I looked out the window to see what the commotion was about. The courtyard was surrounded by children, nuns, and parents. A group of children wearing regional costumes was dancing a Bolivian *cueca,* a folk dance, in the center of the courtyard. Behind them, other classes waited their turn, each wearing a different regional costume. A banner proclaimed the school's twenty-fifth anniversary.

I spotted Michael right away. He and the rest of his class were dressed in the traditional garb of Tarija, Federico's hometown. He looked so cute in his black pants, white shirt, and a hat that kept slipping off his head. One hand was clasped behind his back, and with the other he waved a handkerchief above his head. The little girls wore full skirts and peasant blouses. Each girl wore her hair in two neat braids, with a red rose tucked behind one ear. I watched as the children hopped around to the music in a snaky line. Jane appeared out of the crowd and threw confetti at Michael. Then I saw Federico too. He was taking pictures.

After the dancing came the speeches. I heard the same stock themes and phrases that seemed to be a part of every speech given for any occasion in Bolivia, just as they had performed the same dances, to the same music, and worn the same costumes that I'd seen in a dozen parades and festivals.

Jane and Michael were safe. They were living in an environment where life was slow, predictable, unchanging. On the other hand, I felt frustrated for them. It was a narrow life. They were hemmed in by traditions and fossilized expectations that would end up stifling any creativity they might have, any individuality of thought. I knew that was especially true of Jane, because as a girl her role would be even more confining. She was bright; she could be anything she wanted to be. But if she stayed here those things would never occur to her, much less be encouraged. These little programs of singing and dancing would be the same year after year, and my children would look upon them as the best years of their lives.

After the program was over—Jane's class didn't perform, for some reason—it was announced that in observance of the school's twenty-fifth anniversary, there would be no classes the next day. I groaned inwardly—another long day of waiting lay ahead.

I watched Jane and Michael until they disappeared up the ramp with Federico. As I was blowing my nose and drying my eyes, I heard a key turn in the door. It was Dan, and he was with Roberto. I knew something was wrong from the expressions they wore. Dan avoided my eyes. Roberto sat down and reluctantly began to speak. He explained that Dan and Jennifer had confided in him about my plans and their participation in them. They were worried about being caught and sent home in disgrace. They were also worried about implicating Food Aid International. As Roberto fumbled for words, I decided to help him out.

"What you're trying to say is that they can't do it, right?"

He nodded. "It's not that we don't want to help you, Cassie. But we just can't risk FAI and all our work here."

All I could think was that my best hope for getting Jane and Michael back was being snatched away. I struggled not to cry.

"I understand. Dan, I told you and Jennifer to think about it for those very reasons."

"Jennifer and I really *do* want to help," he insisted. "We think it's the Lord's will for you to get those children back." He turned to Roberto. "You know, it's really pretty unlikely that we'd get caught. After all, what could they say? I wouldn't be doing *anything* . . . just standing there. And afterward Jennifer would slip away and go straight to the office. Who in the world would be able to say that she was the one who helped Cassie? If they got a description of her it would fit every other girl at the school. How could they prove anything?"

"If the police investigated and found out that Cassie was staying in this apartment, they'd check you and Jennifer out pretty carefully," Roberto said. He was Bolivian. He should know.

"How would they find that out? Nobody knows she's here except you and us."

"I think Federico would tell the police about Russ. He knows they've been in touch. They

207

could trace Cassie to this apartment."

"I wish there were some way to get hold of Russ. I think he would want us to help in any way we could," Dan persisted.

Finally Roberto relented. But I had a bad feeling about it.

Later that night, Jennifer knocked softly on my door.

"Can I come in?"

"Sure."

She sat by me on the bed and quietly began. "Cassie, Dan and I have been talking about it. We've decided we can't help after all. There's just too much at stake. Before we came down here, we spent a year going to friends and churches to get pledges to support our work here. We can't let those people down. And we can't risk jeopardizing the whole organization. I hope you understand."

"I do," I said. I didn't want anyone else to suffer for my actions. I had plenty of that on my conscience already.

By now I had moved into the bedroom of Ben and Susanna, who were still in the countryside. After Jennifer left, I lay on the bed and looked out the window at the lights twinkling across the canyon. A neon 7-Up sign on one of the buildings blinked on and off, on and off. All was quiet except for the occasional swish of a car going down the canyon road.

I had never felt so terribly alone. A door had

opened for an instant and I'd glimpsed through it a happy ending to the ordeal. Now it had swung shut. It was time for me to face facts, to face the possibility — no, the *probabililty* — that I would come away from Bolivia empty-handed. Before, in McAllen, I still had other options: the Bolivian courts, a resnatch. But if I failed now, there would be no other options.

I forced myself to contemplate life without Jane and Michael, without even the hope of having them. The reality of it was palpable in the darkened room, like some evil, invisible presence. The pain of it was crushing, suffocating. For hours I lay there unable to move, going down in a descending spiral until at some point in the night, I hit bottom.

Along the way I was stripped of all false optimism, all groundless assumptions that such a thing — sorrow without remedy — could not happen to me. My protective mantle of optimism and my sense of justice were torn away. It *could* happen . . . chances were it *would* happen. Lloyd had as much as said so, and I'd ignored him. His words echoed in my brain: "marginal, very marginal" . . . "never seen so few options" . . . "this plan is the only one that *can* work. . . ."

Strangely enough, my fears had been stripped away along with the false hopes. I felt as though I'd gone through some kind of purification by fire, and had emerged stronger than before. Everything had melted down to one burning purpose: to fight with the last breath in my body to get Jane and Michael back. From that moment on I knew I wouldn't be afraid to risk everything. What was there left to lose? And if I failed, I knew I would somehow go on, and that Jane and Michael would be all right, too.

Chapter Fifteen

Wednesday, April 27, 1988

Everything was quiet at the school. There was no singing or chanting, no band playing, and no children. Around noon Lloyd and Bob arrived laden with food—chunks of raw meat fresh from the open market, cold cuts, crusty rolls of bread, cheese, four bottles of wine, plus the ultimate luxury: paper towels! Bob proudly announced that he'd haggled over the price of the paper towels for ten minutes and gotten it down to five dollars for the roll—a real bargain!

I told them about Dan and Jennifer's decision to back out, and Lloyd's face clouded.

"Well," he said with forced cheerfulness, "we'll try again tomorrow anyway." Then they told me that they had found out that the son of the chief of police attended the school. In fact, the chief had been at the parents' meeting the previous week.

"I imagine he'd be pretty insulted if somebody tried to kidnap a child out of his own son's school," Lloyd said. "He'd probably use all the resources at his disposal to catch whoever dared to do such a thing."

It was much later that I learned *how* they'd found out about the police chief—through the taxi driver they had hired to drive the getaway car. Bob had been telling the driver for several days to be in front of the apartment building at 8:15 A.M., ostensibly to "pick up some people." And afterward Bob would tell him, "Not today after all."

The day before, the taxi driver was parked in front of the building as usual. As he watched the children going into the school, he had idly remarked to Bob, "You're planning to kidnap one of those children, aren't you?" That's when he told Bob about the police chief and his son, and added that the chief was a good friend of his. Lloyd gave the driver enough money to take his wife and family on a vacation for a couple of weeks and threatened to kill him if he returned before then. I didn't know if Lloyd would have carried out his threat, or if it was just talk to scare the taxi driver. I never would have condoned such a thing. In fact, that was one of the conditions I laid down when I first talked to Lloyd: no one was to get hurt. The incident demonstrated how little control I really had over the whole thing.

That morning we discussed the new plan.

"Remember," Lloyd said, "you have no more than thirty seconds to get them out."

I would go down the ramp just ahead of Jane and Michael. Once I was out of sight of the street and around the corner, I'd look up at the window of the apartment for a signal from Lloyd. If Federico walked down with the children, Lloyd would cross his forearms, and I was to hide in the bathroom until the coast was clear. If he didn't, Lloyd would hold up his arms in the signal for a touchdown and I was to go up the ramp and intercept them.

It was simple, and, to my relief, didn't involve the use of two-way radios. I had never felt confident about the radios. For one thing, they were on a frequency that could be overheard on any other short-wave radio within transmitting distance, including those surely found at the Military Police Headquarters just down the street. Second, we didn't know if they would transmit through the thick walls of the school building. Third, I didn't have much faith in technology. What if they malfunctioned at a crucial moment? Too many things could go wrong.

Around six o'clock that night, just as the President returned to his residence down the street amid the sirens of his military escort, Dan and Jennifer arrived. They were delighted with the food that the men had brought. There was no tension from the night before. I didn't harbor any resentment about

213

their decision, and they were kinder than ever, maybe to make up for it.

The next morning I woke up feeling strangely calm. Lloyd arrived and took up his position by the curtains, and we waited for Guy's phone call. He would be watching from the Crillon Hotel for Federico and the children to leave. He called about ten minutes ahead of schedule so we'd be sure to get a telephone line through, always an iffy proposition in La Paz. Lloyd was worried about eavesdroppers listening in, so Guy and I carried on a phony conversation about selling wedding dresses for export—a topic I knew nothing about. Suddenly in mid-sentence the line went dead. I shook the receiver.

"Hello?" I punched the hang-up button repeatedly. Nothing.

"Is anything wrong?" Lloyd asked.

"The line just went dead."

"Try to call him again."

I dialed the hotel again. The operator answered. After a pause, she said, "I'm sorry. I don't know what's wrong, but I can't get a line through to that room. Would you like to leave a message?"

"No, thank you." I hung up and told Lloyd what had happened.

He cursed softly. "We'll wait five minutes and if he doesn't call back, head for the school anyway."

I sat by the phone, tense, as the minutes crawled by. Guy didn't call back. Lloyd looked at his watch.

"Go!"

I was out the door and tripping down the three flights of stairs. Then I started up the driveway to the street, all the while keeping an eye out for Federico or his Jeep. A truck was stopped at the entrance to the street and I couldn't see around it. Finally it turned into the street. The coast was clear. The guard seemed to take no notice as I walked past him. I reached the bottom of the ramp and saw that the children were already lined up to file into the school. I was in plain sight of them. I turned to look up at the window. Lloyd was standing there with his forearms crossed. Abort. I ran quickly down the ten or twelve steps into the schoolyard and darted into the bathroom. Just as I shut myself into the stall at the far end, the bell rang shrilly. Overhead I could hear the children tramping upstairs to class. Then I heard footsteps approaching in the bathroom. There was a sudden rap on the stall door. I froze. The door pushed open—it was Bob.

"Do you have the kids?" he puffed, his face red from exertion. I shook my head. "Come on. Let's get out of here!" and he disappeared out the door.

I peeked outside. Children were still filing past. Michael and Jane could still be out there, and I couldn't risk their seeing me. I waited until the

215

shuffling died down, then as casually as I could, walked back up the ramp. The gate was shut, but the guard was still there. He gave me an incurious glance and opened the gate. I nodded and smiled, *"Gracias."*

My heart thumped. What had gone wrong this time? Back at the apartment, Lloyd explained: just after I'd left the apartment, Federico and the kids had arrived.

"And," Lloyd said, "Federico parked his Jeep at the entrance to the driveway. There was a truck there, and that's why I didn't see him before. He was still there when you came out." He shook his head in disbelief. "If it hadn't been for the truck blocking the way, he'd have seen you."

Lucky break. I only hoped that Jane and Michael hadn't seen me either. I could imagine them going home that day and telling their father, "Guess who we saw today!"

In a few minutes, Bob and Guy joined us. Guy explained that the phone in his hotel room had had a frayed cord for some time. It was a freakish coincidence that it had chosen that moment to finally snap. Lloyd paced the floor.

"Time is running out. We've *got* to pull this off tomorrow. We can't fool around here any longer. Somebody's going to catch on to us." He looked at me. "We'll go for it again in the morning. If it doesn't work then, you'll wait in the bathroom until the ten o'clock morning recess. If you can't

216

do it at recess, then we'll do it after school."

To get them at recess I would have to go into the schoolyard and take them out through the interior of the school, leaving by the front door. The outside gates were kept locked except in the morning when the children arrived and in the afternoon when they left.

"You'll have to tell me how to get from the back door through to the front," I told Bob. In an old building like Amor de Dios, it wouldn't be a straight shoot. He scratched his head.

"There's a whole network of little halls and stairways. And the hell of it is that you'd have to pass by some classrooms too. It would be better if I was waiting inside to lead you and the kids through. Besides, you'll have to pass by the receptionist at the front desk. I could give her some story or try to distract her while you got the kids out."

Lloyd said, "But if for some reason you're not there, she's going to have to know how to do it by herself." He looked at me. "Where's that diagram you drew of the school?"

"In my suitcase. I'll go get it." I smoothed it out on the table. Bob leaned over it.

"Don't touch it," Lloyd warned him. "We can't leave our fingerprints on anything. If somebody gets hold of this, the only thing they'll find is Cassie's fingerprints. Nobody's to know we were ever here."

217

Pointing with a pencil Bob traced a route up the back stairs and through the school. He gave me the pencil and I drew in stairs and hallways where he indicated them.

"Okay, if we have to do it after school, we can go through the gate. That'll be tricky, though. Federico always arrives before the children get out of school, and he waits outside for them. He'd have to be delayed somehow." Lloyd took the pencil and drew a line from the schoolyard and along the south wall of the school, the opposite side from the ramp they usually went up and down.

"There's a gate on that side, too, but nobody ever seems to use it. There's no guard there. We need to find out if it's kept locked or not. If you can come down this ramp and intercept the children when they come out of school for recess," he drew an invisible line with the pencil eraser, "then you can leave by going up the ramp on the other side of the school. He won't be looking for them there."

"But everybody will see me do it. All the teachers and kids will be out in the courtyard, too."

Lloyd set the pencil down. "Well, we don't have a whole lot of options at this point. If it comes to that, we'll just have to do it that way."

I nodded. But my stomach was in knots.

After they left, and against Lloyd's instructions, I called my father.

"Cassie! Where are you calling from?"

It was so good to hear his voice! He and the world I'd left a few days ago seemed light years away.

"We all want to know what's going on. Your brothers and grandmother have been calling." When I'd left McAllen, I'd told Daddy I'd be gone only a couple of days. That had been eleven days ago.

"Daddy, nothing's happening right now. We've already tried to get them twice and couldn't. But tomorrow is *the* day. I'll either get Jane and Michael back tomorrow or my next phone call will be from prison," I joked.

He didn't laugh. "When are we going to know something?"

"Don't expect to hear from me for at least a couple of days. If we get Jane and Michael, I won't be able to make any phone calls until we're safely out of Bolivia." I didn't tell him how slim our chances were.

"Okay. Be careful. I love you."

"I love you, too, Daddy." It was hard to hang up, to give up that tie to home and safety.

Later that morning I watched Jane and Michael at recess. They rushed toward each other and hugged happily, then ran to slide down a banister. The other kids paid no attention to them. They were foreigners here, different, and in all likelihood didn't fit in. Michael was probably too young to care, but being shut out would cause Jane a lot of pain. For the umpteenth time, I was thankful they were close.

I remembered hearing them talking to each other at night after they were in bed. They'd discuss the events of the day, and sometimes they'd have giggle fits over something. Michael would ask Jane things like why do tennis balls have hair, and she'd dispense her big sister wisdom on the subject.

I wondered what they talked to each other about now, in the dark, cold nights.

After lunch Roberto paid me another visit. This time he came alone. He sat down uncomfortably and began talking again about the predicament that FAI would be in should the police investigate and find out that I had used the FAI apartment as our base of operations. It was clear what was coming next. Once again I helped him out.

"What you're trying to say is I have to leave." He nodded unhappily. And once again I told Roberto that I understood. The script of the day before was played out again, but this time I was being kicked out. He asked me to leave by evening, wished me luck, and left.

I didn't see any reason to wait around until evening. I didn't want to be there when Dan and Jennifer returned for lunch, didn't want to see their apologetic faces or hear any more explanations. I was tired of sympathy. I threw my few things together and then called Lloyd.

"I need to leave here. Right now. As soon as you can come get me."

He didn't ask any questions. "We'll be right there."

I was angry. I had never asked for their help, but Dan and Jennifer had volunteered it. Then, as soon as they'd realized that there *were* risks involved—risks I'd warned them about in the first place—they'd backed out. Once again our plans were thrown out of kilter and would have to be reworked. My chances of getting Jane and Michael back seemed more remote than ever.

I took my small gray duffle bag in one hand and snatched up my purse and jacket in the other, leaving behind my suitcase, along with some clothes and other dispensable items. I took one last look at the school. Then I locked the door behind me and went downstairs to wait, sitting on the curb in the parking lot.

In a few minutes Bob drove up and bounded out, a big smile on his face. He hugged me, then took my bag. He didn't have to ask what had happened.

"It's okay. This is just a minor setback," he winked. "You've still got us, and we haven't failed yet."

I slid onto the backseat next to Guy. He patted

my arm and said, "We're gonna get those kids back."

Even Lloyd was trying to be optimistic. "The apartment doesn't really matter. We're just back to our original plan, that's all."

We drove across town to the Hotel Gloria, where Bob checked me in under his name. Then we had lunch in the top-floor restaurant. The men chatted about the city.

I was sitting with my back to the other diners in the restaurant. I glanced around. Businessmen would be arriving soon for lunch. Even with my wig on, I felt publicly exposed, open to discovery at any moment. But the men were in no hurry to leave.

Lloyd began discussing plans for the following morning. This time, without the apartment to signal from, we would have to use the two-way radios. And they had arranged for a Bolivian girl to dress in a school uniform and intercept Jane and Michael on the ramp. Bob and Lloyd began arguing about the details.

Guy gave me a weary smile. "Boy, I get tired of listening to those two."

Finally, lunch over, Bob and I took the elevator down a few floors to my room which was registered under Bob's name. How many rooms had I stayed in since arriving in La Paz, I wondered. I'd lost count. The room was small and chilly, but it had a carpet, and the bathroom fixtures were

222

modern.

As soon as Bob left, I looked for a heater or thermostat. There were none. The Hotel Gloria was in a higher part of town than the Sheraton or the FAI apartment, and with each meter of altitude the temperature dropped accordingly. I called room service to ask about the advertised central heating and to request an extra blanket. A security guard posing as a maintenance man came and poked around the room, ostensibly to turn on the heat. He kept glancing at me out of the corner of his eyes. When he asked where Sr. Kreiler was, I gave him the secretarial story that Bob and I had agreed on earlier. It seemed plausible enough; I was sitting on the bed surrounded by papers and writing on a tablet. I answered his questions. Yes, Mr. Kreiler was staying there alone. No, I would *not* be spending the night. The guard left, apparently satisfied with my story. He didn't come back.

Lloyd was supposed to come by later to get me something to eat. As the evening wore on, I climbed under the bedcovers and the extra blanket and tried to concentrate on the mystery novel I'd bought in Miami. The hours ticked by. The room darkened. At one point the electricity went off for about thirty minutes. I went to the window. An entire section of town was blacked out. Then, just as inexplicably as they'd gone off, the lights came back on.

It was almost midnight when Lloyd finally arrived. (Later, I learned why it always took him so long; he'd sometimes spend hours walking around losing "tails." The Bolivian undercover agents may not have been subtle, but they were very persistent.)

We went to the hotel coffee shop—the restaurant was closed by that hour. As I sipped coca tea to calm my stomach, which was twisting in anticipation of what lay ahead, Lloyd waxed garrulous. He was definitely a night person. The later it got, the more he seemed to relax and loosen up. He told me very interesting things about his career in the FBI—things I promised never to reveal—and about his current job as the head of a private investigation firm. We got onto more personal topics, like what makes for a happy marriage and even what type of diet he was on.

It was well into the morning when I finally crawled into bed.

Chapter Sixteen

Friday, April 29, 1988

Bob forgot to give me a wake-up call, but I woke up at the appointed time anyway. It was 6:20 A.M. I dressed in my traveling clothes—faithful old jeans, white knit shirt—and then brushed my hair. This time I wouldn't be wearing the wig, at least until we got Jane and Michael. I packed my duffle bag and then waited for Bob. He knocked on the door just before 8 A.M.

The Blazer was parked down the block. Waiting inside was Karina, the Bolivian teenager who was going to help us. She was already dressed in the white school uniform. Bob tossed a two-way radio into my lap and started to explain how to operate it as he began to drive. Morning rush-hour traffic was in full swing.

"Gotta get gas first. I was in line last night to buy some and they ran out before they got to me," he griped. "Anyway"—he was talking fast, in Spanish and English, so neither Karina nor I would miss anything—"about the radios, as soon as you get into the bathroom, I'll time it. I'll test them to make sure they'll work through those walls." He honked the horn and nosed into the next lane. "I'll say, 'Testing, one-two-three,' and then you push down the red button and say, 'Four-five-six,' and that way I'll know you can hear me."

I turned the radio over in my hands, but my mind was still on Bob's first comment. Gas? Why now, of all times, were we caught low on gas?

"Where am I supposed to put this so nobody will see it?" I asked. And why didn't we go over all this before? I thought nervously as I examined the little buttons on the transmitter. It wasn't much bigger than a package of cigarettes.

"Put the earpiece in your ear, then run the wire under your clothes. You can hook the transmitter onto your jeans. Nobody'll see it under your jacket." I rigged myself up as he said.

Bob pulled into line at the gas station. The man in front of us, his tank already filled, was having a leisurely chat with the attendant. Bob flung open his door and yelled, *"Apurese!* Hurry up!"

Looking back at me in the rearview mirror, he continued, "This is the signal: If Federico comes down the ramp with the kids, I won't say anything. You just wait there in the bathroom until the morning recess. If the kids come down alone, I'll say 'solo.' In that case, sit tight for a few seconds to give Federico time to start leaving. Then wait until

226

you hear me say 'ven' (*come*). That means haul out of there and get those kids. In the meantime, Karina here will intercept them on the ramp until you can get to them."

My heart was pounding. As the attendant put gas in the Blazer, I went over and over the plans in my mind. Finally Bob pulled into traffic again. We were on the busiest street downtown and still had several miles to go to the school. Bob ran a red light; the traffic police blew the whistle and came running after us.

"Damn," Bob muttered as he pulled to the side of the street. He rolled down his window, smiled, and put on his dumb tourist act. Surprisingly, the policeman didn't insist that Bob go to the police station to pay a fine—he didn't even hint around for a bribe. He let him go with a short lecture.

"Gracias!" Bob pulled into the line of cars again. I glanced at my watch. It was 8:10. Federico would be leaving the apartment with the children in five minutes. The streets thronged with people, buses, cars, and taxis. The air reverberated with the sound of honking horns. Traffic crawled. The thought came to me again that maybe it just wasn't meant to be. Things weren't going right.

Finally we neared the edge of downtown, and the streets cleared. We were close now. We drove past Guy, who was standing on a street corner. He was stationed there to watch for Federico and, when he drove by, to signal Lloyd by radio.

"Good," Bob breathed, "That means Federico

hasn't driven by yet. We're in luck—he's running late." He looked at me in the rearview mirror. "As soon as I pull up, you jump out and get down that ramp as fast as you can. He must be right behind us."

White-smocked children were clustered around candy stands at the gate. I slipped past the guard and pushed through the knots of schoolgirls on the ramp—around the corner, down the steps, and into the open door of the bathroom. The walls echoed with the chattering and giggling of the older girls primping in front of the mirrors. No one seemed to notice as I slipped into the stall nearest the door. I pressed one finger to my ear and strained to listen to the earphone hidden under my hair. Nothing. Bob wasn't testing the radio, or—a worse thought— it wasn't transmitting through the thick walls.

The bell rang and the chattering died away as the bathroom emptied. Outside, the children's voices piped up in the first strains of the national anthem. That meant they were already in their lines. Did we miss Jane and Michael? What happened to Bob? The radio was still silent. Visions of crouching in the stall for two more hours flashed through my mind. My guts twisted like a wrung-out dischcloth.

Suddenly the radio crackled and through the static I heard the word "Solo." I forgot about waiting for his next signal. Heart racing, I flung myself out of the stall and out the door and—Dear God, there they were! on the landing with Karina!—I don't remember going up the stairs but there I was,

228

kneeling in front of them laughing and crying and saying their names over and over. Jane's look of puzzlement turned to astonishment when she saw me.

"Mommy!" she cried. "What are you doing here?"

"I came to see you," I laughed. Michael stared at the ground. His lower lip was thrust out and quivering.

"Michael, it's me, *Mommy,*" I said. He lifted his gaze and studied my face for a moment, then broke into a smile. "Mommy!" he echoed. I talked fast as I took their hands and started up the ramp.

"I came to see you. We're going to the car to get the presents I brought you. You've grown so much! You're so big! I've missed you so much," I rattled on. The ramp was deserted except for a nun standing near the top. As I passed she put her hand on my arm.

"You can't take these children without their father's permission."

I brazened a smile and kept walking. *"Momentito."* But the gate had swung shut and the guard stood there unmoving. I stopped, still clutching the children's hands. Bob pushed his way through from the other side. Waving the brown envelope that held the letter to the Mother Superior and the sheaf of legal documents, he began to argue with the nun. He told her that I was their mother, that it was all legal. But she refused to take the envelope and kept shaking her head, saying, "You can't take these children! You have to go inside and speak with the Mother Superior!"

Somehow in the confusion Michael had slipped out of my grasp. Panicked, I glanced around. He wasn't with Karina—she was standing outside the gate. I looked the other way—he was heading back down the ramp and looking back at me, his face contorted with imminent tears. No! I thought, I can't leave him behind.

"Michael, come back!" I yelled.

His face brightened. He scurried back up the ramp, grabbed my hand, and proudly announced to the nun, *"Esta es mi mama!* This is my mommy!"

The nun hesitated, confused. She looked at Bob, then at me, then threw up her hands. "Take them! I don't want to be a part of it!" She turned her back and started hobbling back down the ramp.

Incredibly, the guard swung the gate open. I forced myself to walk, not run, to the Blazer. Oh God, it was happening. We were going to get away with it. I pushed Jane and Michael into the back seat of the Blazer and jumped in after them. Bob took off driving, Karina beside him in the front seat. Lloyd and Bob followed in a Jeep. It was 8:25 A.M.

Jane and Michael sat still, eyes wide.

"What about school?" Jane asked. "We'll miss school."

"You won't be going back to school today," I said.

"Where are we going?" she asked.

"We're going home."

"Home to Daddy or home to Texas?" she asked.

"Where do you want to go?" I asked and tensed for her reply.

"Texas," she answered firmly.

"Are you sure?"

"Yes."

Up to now Michael had been silent. Now he said gravely, "Daddy shouldn't have taken us away."

I pulled a black sweater over my white shirt and put the wig on, explaining to the kids that I would look funny for a while. I kept chattering cheerfully as I took off their school clothes, layer after layer of them, and dressed them in the blue jeans and jackets I had brought. The hood on Jane's jacket covered up her blonde hair, and Michael's knit cap covered his head. They still looked like little gringos, but without their hair showing it wouldn't be so obvious. Then for a few blocks I had them lie down on the seat out of sight. I stroked their heads in my lap and kept talking.

Bob cursed as he maneuvered through the narrow serpentine streets in the Indian section of La Paz, well away from the main thoroughfares of the city. The open markets went on for blocks and the streets teemed with people and honking cars. My imagination had never gone beyond the act of getting the kids out of the school; I always assumed that if we got that far, we were home free. But now I realized that our journey was just beginning. Bob was obviously trying to reach El Alto by back roads. At a crowded intersection, he started to turn left and the traffic cop blew his whistle.

"There's no left turn allowed here," said Karina.

Bob cursed. He rolled down his window. *"Por favor!"* he begged, but the policeman shook his head and motioned Bob to continue straight ahead.

"You're supposed to be giving me directions out of here!" Bob snapped at Karina. "Now what?"

Karina began pointing the way, but didn't seem so sure herself. I glanced behind us. Guy was driving the white Jeep with Lloyd beside him. Lloyd grinned and gave me the circled thumb and forefinger "A-OK" signal. Twenty minutes later we had snaked our way up the sides of the canyon until we reached a bluff overlooking the city. Bob pulled the Blazer onto the gravel shoulder, and we piled out to switch to the Jeep. In the general scrambling Jane's name tag fell face up in the dust by the road.

To Guy I gave a quick hug good-bye and to Karina a hurried *"Gracias!"* They got into the Blazer. Guy would fly out of La Paz and be on his way to Miami the following morning. Bob took the driver's seat in the Jeep, and Lloyd sat beside him. The Jeep was smaller and more cramped than the Blazer. The space behind the front seat was crammed with Lloyd's and Bob's bags and parcels. I sat down on one of the two facing bench seats and settled Jane and Michael on the floor, where they couldn't be seen from outside.

Moments later we were driving among the adobe slums of El Alto. On both sides of the road open ditches carried raw sewage. Behind those squatted the mud houses of country peasants who had come to the city hoping for a better life. The streets were under construction in preparation for the Pope's visit, and Bob groaned as he negotiated the poorly marked detours. But by taking the back roads he had managed to avoid the toll booths on the main road. In minutes we were on the paved highway leading to Lake Titicaca, an hour and a half away. Before then I didn't know whether the plan was to leave Bolivia by air or by land. I could see that we weren't headed for the airport.

"I guess this means we're not taking a plane," I said to Lloyd.

"The airport has been out of the question for a long time," he said. He explained that they'd separately contracted two different private planes to take us into Peru. But the planes could be called back by radio even after they were in the air. Besides, the pilots couldn't be relied upon. On a trial run, Lloyd said that he and Bob had reached the airport only to find that neither the planes nor the pilots were ready. Such a delay would be disastrous—the airport would be the first place they'd look for us.

Meanwhile, the children's apprehension had dissolved and they were chattering away—in English but with unmistakable Spanish accents—and singing songs in Spanish. I drank it in. I couldn't believe that the objects of my longing and anguish for the past six months were finally sitting there before me. How precious they were! I had forgotten the funny way Jane pursed her lips like Shirley Temple when she talked, and how wide and green Michael's eyes were. Every few minutes he would kiss my hand and press it to his face, declaring, "Mommy, I love you." Then he and Jane would hug each other in unrestrained joy.

Sometime in that first hour on the road I explained to them that their Daddy had kidnapped them—taken them away without my knowing it. Jane said that when they left McAllen, Federico had told them that they were going to visit their *abuelita,* like they'd done in July.

With childlike honesty Michael said, "Sometimes I forgot about you. Then I'd remember you and cry. Then I'd forget again."

"Did your daddy say why he took you away?" I asked.

Jane answered, "He said you were with a bad guy."

"Yeah," confirmed Michael. "He said the bad guy would put poison in our cereal."

Good Lord, I thought.

Then we talked about the event of the morning.

"Mommy, I was surprised to see you at school," Jane said.

"Me, too," said Michael. "At first I didn't remember who you were. But then I remembered," he smiled.

"Why were you going back down the sidewalk?" I asked him.

"The teacher yelled at me to go back to my class.

I was afraid you were going to leave without me."

I hugged him, "I wouldn't have left without you."

"I thought she was mad at me."

"She was mad all right, but not at you, honey."

From the duffle bag I dug out the presents I had brought for them. The gift wrap was a bit rumpled, but they didn't notice. They were delighted with their gifts: a Skipper doll for Jane and a transformer toy for Michael.

I tried to keep them unaware of the tension in the Jeep. I told them we were going to take a fun trip and would play a lot of games. As we approached the first police checkpoint, I covered them with Lloyd's trench coat and told them about the first game: they were rabbits hiding from a wolf—the little rabbits had to lie very still and quiet so the wolf wouldn't find them. They cooperated with enthusiasm and sat motionless under the coat as Bob showed the police his documents. The police waved us on without checking inside the Jeep.

As we drove on toward Lake Titicaca, passing by peasant villages and fields of maize and horsebeans, Jane and Michael dozed off. I listened apprehensively as Lloyd and Bob argued about which route to take into Peru. It sounded like the hydrofoil—my personal favorite—was out of the running. Who could have caught us skimming the water at 100 miles per hour in the middle of the lake? We'd be on the Peruvian side in an hour. But the hydrofoils, like the planes, were tied by radio to La Paz and they, too, could be called back. Lloyd had left a reservation at the hydrofoil agency anyway, as a red herring—just as he'd told me to make reservations to Miami on Eastern Airlines for a week from now. Maybe they'd think we were hiding out in Bolivia until then.

Now they were arguing about which border town to use to cross into Peru. Why hadn't they decided that earlier? I wondered. They were saying that the village of Desaguadero was farther away than Copacabana, but Bob knew the captain of immigration there. On the other hand, we would have to pass through a military fort on the way. And Copacabana? If it was a market day, the border would be swarming with vendors crossing back and forth, and border security would be lax. But what if it wasn't market day? They ended up going with Copacabana.

By now we had reached the edge of Lake Titicaca, its sparkling blue waters surrounded by the distant snowy peaks of the Andes Mountains. The reed boats of the Indians dotted its banks, and on shore, women and children toiled in fields and tended sheep.

"Let's get rid of these," Lloyd said, and grabbed the children's discarded school clothes. Bob pulled to the side of the road. Lloyd took the little bundle of clothes and the children's book bags and dumped them over a low mud fence. He made an incongruous figure in his impeccable gray suit, leaping puddles among the mud huts.

A little farther on we reached the Strait of Tiquina, the narrowest crossing point on the lake, where wooden ferries would take us across. On the other side was the Bolivian naval base at Tiquina. Bob pulled the Jeep onto the loading ramp. Jane and Michael were still asleep under their "tent." As the returning ferry neared shore, a stern-faced man in a black uniform approached and rapped on Bob's window. He demanded that Bob come inside the post.

"What's the problem?" Bob asked. The guard repeated that he'd have to come inside, so Bob followed him into the building. I waited, scarcely breathing, as the seconds ticked by. Maybe the police had been alerted and I would have to hand Jane and Michael over here. Five long minutes later, Bob returned.

"Whew," he sighed heavily as he climbed back into the Jeep. "All they wanted was the crossing fee." By now the ferry was waiting for us, and Bob guided the Jeep onto its wooden planks. The Jeep rocked gently as we crossed the Strait. Jane and Michael woke up and threw off the coat.

"Mommy, where are we? We want to look outside."

Lloyd said sharply. "Keep them covered up."

I replaced the coat. "We're crossing the lake right now. When we get to the other side, I'll tell you when you can sit up and look."

On the other side Bob drove the Jeep off the ferry and maneuvered it through the rutted muddy roads of the tiny naval base. It looked like just another lakeside village except that everywhere you looked there were black-uniformed sailors. Before leaving the base we stopped once more at a checkpoint. Bob jumped out of the Jeep and went inside before anyone had a chance to come to us. He quickly returned.

"No problem," he said cheerily. "As soon as we clear the edge of town, you can tell the kids to sit up."

Then we were on our way to Copacabana. The day was warming up. Eucalyptus trees towered over the road, shading it from the bright sun. Jane and Michael stretched, sat up, and looked around. Michael took a seat next to me. Every few minutes he would press my hand and say, "I'm glad you came, Mommy."

For the next two hours we wound our way through the hilly countryside on a twisting dirt road. This road, like most in Bolivia, allowed passage for only one vehicle at a time. It was the custom to honk at each bend to warn oncoming cars. When two cars approached from opposite directions, one would pull close to the outside edge of the road, usually within inches of a dangerous precipice, and the other would edge by on the inside. This system didn't always work, however, as evidenced by the many roadside crosses marking fatalities. Road trips in Bolivia were not for the white-knuckled traveler.

About an hour outside Tiquina, a ragged peasant appeared in the middle of the road. He took up a belligerent stance and refused to let us pass until we gave him money. Bob grumbled, but tossed him a coin. The beggar doffed his hat and stepped aside.

It was 12:30 P.M. when we approached the checkpoint on the outskirts of Copacabana. A chain strung across the road barred the way. By this time the children had fallen asleep again. I made sure they were well covered up. Bob jumped out of the Jeep and went inside the dingy green shack. Through the dusty window I could see him gesturing and waving a bill in his hand. There was some hitch, it seemed, and as before, each minute he was inside seemed an hour. He finally returned, explaining that they were demanding some kind of pass that we should have been given at the first checkpoint. A small bribe had taken care of it.

Copacabana's dusty roads were all but deserted. Obviously it was not a market day. Too bad we didn't arrive on a Saturday or Sunday, either. Every weekend Bolivians and Peruvians alike, in a synthesis of ancient pagan rites and Catholicism, draped their new cars with flowers and streamers and drove them to Copacabana to be blessed by the Virgin. But none of this activity was in evidence today.

Bob parked the Jeep a couple of hundred feet down the road from one of the two border crossings in town.

"I'll go in by myself first and sniff out the situation. If it doesn't seem like they've heard anything, I'll try to get entry visas for all five of us and permission to drive the Jeep across to Peru."

239

"Okay," Lloyd said. "But if something doesn't seem right, don't mention the kids at all."

After Bob left, I asked, "If we don't get their passports stamped, then how are we going to get Jane and Michael into Peru?"

"We'll have to smuggle them in somehow." Lloyd glanced into the back of the Jeep and said sharply, "Keep those children covered up."

I did as he said, although by now the afternoon sun beating through the windows was quite warm. The children slept on. As we waited for Bob, I watched as a lone figure in a leather jacket ambled up the street toward us. He seemed to look inside the Jeep with more than casual interest. Then he headed for the immigration building and disappeared inside.

After twenty minutes or so Bob came out with a few other men. One of them was the man in the leather jacket. They walked toward the car and then stopped some thirty yards away. After talking with them a few minutes more, Bob shook hands all around and came back to the Jeep.

"I don't know," he shook his head. "I have a bad feeling about those guys. I didn't show them the kids' passports." He said that the whole time he was inside, one of the men had been watching the Jeep through binoculars. "I hope you kept the kids down," he said, " 'cause they were sure looking for *something*." He told us that the man in the leather jacket was in charge of the post. My heart pounded. That was a close one.

Now we had reached the most critical part of the journey: getting the children out of Bolivia. Once we were inside Peru, I thought, then we'd be safe. My stomach churned.

Bob drove along the lake lined with fishing boats, and he and Lloyd discussed our options. Nearby was the hill where the twelve stations of the Cross were set up for religious pilgrims. Bob stopped the Jeep and he and Lloyd gazed at it. Hundreds of steps led up through the stations of the Cross to the summit. Peru lay on the other side.

Lloyd asked me, "Do you think you could walk up that hill and over to the other side with the kids? You could wait by the roadside for me and Bob. We could cross over through the regular border crossing and pick you up in the Jeep."

"I guess so. But what if somebody stopped and questioned me? It would be pretty hard to explain what I was doing there."

"She's right, Lloyd. And we wouldn't be around to help if something were to happen."

They discarded that idea. Finally they decided that our best shot would be to cross the border in a crowded van-sized taxi. They were betting that the more passengers it had, the less carefully its occupants and their papers would be scrutinized.

So, I thought, it had all come down to this: after all the weeks of careful planning and watching, in the end it came down to a toss of the dice. And if we lost? My chest seemed to squeeze in on itself and I couldn't get my breath for a few seconds. I looked at the children. They slept on. I took a few deep breaths to try to calm my wildly beating heart.

Bob drove to a small plaza where taxis of all sizes were filling with passengers. Bob approached the young driver of a taxi-van, and after some negotiating, he nodded. We all got out of the Jeep. The children had awoken by now and were happy to stretch their legs. Lloyd and Bob piled their luggage into an open area in the back of the van. Quickly I lay Jane across the last seat in the rear of the van. I piled some bundles into the cramped space on the floor between the seats and lay Michael on top of those. I whispered urgently, "Just for a little while longer you have to be *very* still and quiet. It's very important to do as I say now."

Wide-eyed and serious, they obeyed without a word. Michael's head was jammed against the side of the van at an uncomfortable angle, but he looked up at me with complete trust in his eyes. With shaking hands I stuffed my purse under his neck.

The van was quickly filling up with other passengers; Lloyd and Bob took their seats among them. I turned back to the kids and whispered again, "Just for a *little* while longer—don't move and don't say anything, even a whisper. Remember, like little rabbits." I covered them both with Lloyd's trenchcoat. With one hand I began to pat Jane's rigid body, and under the corner of the coat Michael clung to my other hand.

242

The van was now full, mostly with Indian women with babies on their backs and bundles in their arms. We lurched to a start and I began a desperate prayer. In less than a minute we were at the border crossing. Two black-jacketed border guards approached. The taxi driver produced the passports of his passengers—except Jane's and Michael's, which he didn't have. He knew they were in his van. He had watched them board. He said nothing.

I recognized one of the guards; he had been at the first border crossing. When he saw Bob he raised his eyebrows questioningly.

Bob shrugged and shouted amiably, "We decided not to take the Jeep across after all." The guard continued to look through the passengers' documents.

Meanwhile the other guard strolled around to the back of the van. He shouted to his partner in Spanish, "Maybe these people are the ones with the two kids."

My blood seemed to freeze in my veins. Had I heard right? Bob threw me an inscrutable glance over his shoulder. Had he heard it too?

The guard flung open the back doors of the van and surveyed it slowly. I tried to look nonchalant, unconcerned, even as my heart seemed to be bursting out of my chest. He began patting the luggage. Directly under his nose, Jane's shoe was peeking out from under Lloyd's coat. The guard didn't look down. He didn't touch Lloyd's coat. The children didn't stir. He gave one long last look, slammed the

243

doors shut and waved us through. The van started up.

Elation and disbelief swept through me. Lloyd looked back and nodded almost imperceptibly. Bob winked.

I leaned over Jane's and Michael's still bodies. "You're brave little soldiers!" I whispered. "Now it'll be just a little while longer!" It wasn't over yet. Now we were crossing a no-man's land between the borders of Peru and Bolivia, a rocky dirt road that made the children bounce up and down on the hard seats.

After a while Michael said in a small voice, "Mommy, my neck hurts. I can't stand it much longer."

"Just a little bit longer, just a little bit," I kept saying. Almost six hours had passed since we'd left the school that morning. Jane and Michael were tired, cramped, and probably hungry, yet they hadn't complained or questioned anything I'd told them to do. It was miraculous—Michael was never still for longer than five minutes, unless he was asleep, and Jane was not one to suffer discomfort in silence. Yet they had borne up with amazing courage and fortitude. Somehow they must have sensed the urgency of the situation.

We still had to get through the border crossing on the Peruvian side. There we would have to get the children's passports stamped in order for them to enter Peru legally. If we didn't, we'd run into problems when we tried to leave the country.

Please, I prayed, just let us get inside Peru. Then we'll be safe. After all, Peru was Bob's stomping grounds. He'd assured us that he could handle just about anything there. He had lived in Peru off and on for years and still owned a house in the city of Trujillo.

Finally we jolted to a halt at the Peruvian border station. A guard sauntered to the van and stood looking through the window directly across from me. By now Jane and Michael were squirming visibly under the coat. I stared back at him helplessly. For what seemed like the hundredth time that day I thought, "This is it. The game's up." But Bob had already sized up the situation. He bounced out of the van and began a stream of chatter with the guard. Then he casually glanced at the wriggling coat and said, "Ah, veo que los ninos han despertado. Oh, I see the children have waked up," then kept on talking. The guard showed no more interest and walked away.

This time Bob took all five passports into the station. Minutes ticked by. I fought back a wave of nausea. If they didn't approve of our documents, they'd notify Bolivia and send us right back. After another eternity, Bob emerged, jubilant, waving the passports.

"I can't believe our luck! The chief of this station is an old friend of mine." Bob had worked with him in the past on what he called "other projects," in northern Peru. We were in the southeastern part of Peru, hundreds of miles from where they'd last

245

seen each other.

"I put all the passports on the desk and then I laid a five dollar bill on top of each one," Bob explained. "My amigo was tickled pink—said he hadn't seen that much money in months! He stamped the passports without looking at the names. He didn't even register us in the logbook."

That meant there would be no record that Jane and Michael had ever left Bolivia or entered Peru.

I watched out the back of the van until the border post became a speck in the distance. Then Bob turned and shouted, "Let those kids up!" I looked questioningly at Lloyd and he smiled and nodded. I threw off the trench coat covering Jane and Michael. They sat up, rubbing their eyes in the sunlight, and looked around.

"Where are we?"

"We're in Peru!" If I'd said "the promised land" the words couldn't have been sweeter. I hugged them until their ribs creaked. After their long enforced silence, within minutes they were chattering like magpies. Lloyd looked back at us with a benign smile on his face. Bob grinned.

Chapter Seventeen

Roads in Peru were paved and in a much better condition than the ones in Bolivia, so it wasn't long before we were deposited on the sleepy main square of Yunguyo, a small market town. We unloaded ourselves and our luggage onto the dusty sidewalk. It was 2:30 P.M. Bob and I hugged.

"Didn't I tell you we'd do it?" he chuckled.

Lloyd wiped his mouth on his sleeve, took me by the shoulders, and planted a kiss squarely on my mouth.

The men stayed at the plaza to wait for the next form of transportation—be it taxi, bus, or vegetable truck—that could take us to the town of Puno, where there was an airport with flights to Lima. In the meantime Jane, Michael, and I walked to a little store down the street. We were hungry and thirsty—we hadn't eaten since early that morning. A tiny girl no bigger than Jane waited on us. Three men drinking beer at a corner table watched us with bleary-eyed interest. We sat on the curb outside the store with our cookies and Cokes. Jane gave some of her cookies to a street urchin standing nearby. Lloyd strolled over.

"You and the children better stay inside where nobody can see you. It might take a while for us to get out of here. We could've been followed."

We retreated to the dim interior of the store. I sat at a small oilcloth-covered table and felt my body go limp as all the tension built up from the past few hours drained away. Jane and Michael, illuminated by a shaft of sunlight slanting in the door, laughed and jumped at moths in the swirling dust motes. Every few minutes they hugged each other. I was bursting with joy and pride, and with the knowledge of having been unbelievably lucky. No, it was more than luck. As I sat there watching my children, I had the sense that I had been the recipient of some kind of unearthly grace—that for some unfathomable reason I had been granted an immense and wholly undeserved favor. By all odds, events should not have happened as they did.

It took about an hour for transportation to arrive, this time a tour van headed for Puno. Once in the van, Bob told me to relax and take off my wig for a while, and I did, to the delight of Jane and Michael. An Indian girl stared at me across her mother's shoulder. Bob befriended the driver and his brother and offered them thirty dollars extra if they'd take us to Juliaca, a somewhat larger city a few miles beyond Puno, and one, presumably, where we'd have a better chance of getting a flight to Lima. They agreed immediately—thirty dollars was probably a week's earnings to them. On the way Jane and Michael played and bounced around on the empty seats. Jane made a bed for her new Skipper doll out of a sheet of newspaper. Lloyd held Michael in his lap. We were all in high spirits.

We arrived in Juliaca at 6 P.M. At the Aeroperu office Bob was informed that all flights to Lima were booked until Monday. We'd have to stay overnight in Juliaca. Our helpful drivers located for us the only available hotel room in town.

We checked in and were led upstairs to our room. Our footsteps echoed on the wooden floors. Lloyd set his huge duffle bag down and surveyed the room. There were two single beds, a small nightstand, a sink in the corner (no towels or soap), a wooden chair, and an old-fashioned wooden wardrobe. Bathrooms were down the hall. The two lumpy beds looked wonderful. I fell across one and the children snuggled against me on either side.

"Okay, this is what we're going to do," Lloyd said, sitting in the chair with a weary sigh. "You can have one of the beds and the children can sleep in the other—"

"No," Michael said, "I wanna sleep with Mommy!"

"Me too!" echoed Jane.

Bob said to Lloyd, "We could sleep on the sofa in the lobby."

"Nope. We're gonna sleep on the floor right here. I don't want them out of my sight."

Bob looked dubiously at the hardwood floors but said gamely, "The floor'll be fine."

We were all starving. Next door to the hotel was an

open-air cafe. The menu was simple: greasy chicken and french fries, and the local soda pop. Lloyd was uneasy.

"We need to keep moving. I feel like we're sitting ducks. Let's see if we can get train tickets out of here."

From where we sat we could see the train station, just across the main plaza from the cafe. People were queued up the length of a block to buy tickets for the night train, even though the ticket office had not yet opened.

"The next train leaves tonight at nine and it arrives in Arequipa at eight in the morning. If we could get to Arequipa we'd have a better chance of flying to Lima. It has a bigger airport and more airlines," Bob said.

The night train to Arequipa . . . it sounded familiar. Then I remembered—I'd read about it in one of the travel books in Dan and Jennifer's apartment. Theft was rampant throughout Peru, but the night train to Arequipa was notorious for thievery. The book warned, "Don't close your eyes during the night, or you could wake up to find all your possessions gone. If you travel in a group, take turns keeping watch." Even more disquieting, I remembered the travel advisories posted in the consulate: the terrorist group Sendero Luminoso, "Shining Path," was active throughout the Arequipa province.

Bob said he'd try to get us train tickets as soon as he finished his meal. As we ate, he kept an eye on the people passing by the open front of the cafe. Suddenly he leaped up and exclaimed, "There's the guy I'm looking for!" and was gone.

Lloyd shook his head. "Count on Bob to see somebody he knows even in a godforsaken place like this. And you know what? I'll bet you anything he gets those damn tickets." I was doubtful. Across the plaza the line at the ticket stand had grown longer.

I took Jane and Michael to the filthy latrine at the back of the restaurant, grateful that I had a supply of Kleenex with me. I knew there wouldn't be any toilet paper. As we were coming back, wading through a murky liquid covering the floor, the lights went out. We made our way back to our table in the dark. People continued to eat unconcernedly during the twenty minutes or so it took for the lights to come back on.

Jane and Michael cleaned their plates. As we tried to wipe our fingers on the inadequate scraps of tissue paper that passed as napkins, Bob returned, grinning and waving five train tickets. He had wangled them from three different people waiting in line, since the ticket seller allowed only two tickets per person.

We crossed to the plaza, where I bought several wool and alpaca sweaters from sidewalk vendors. I knew that the crossing through the Andes would be bitterly cold. An Indian woman hounded Bob into buying a beautiful alpaca rug from her for $20.

Back at the hotel, the men tried to arrange their bulky luggage into more manageable bundles. I discarded yet more of my things, bequeathing to that nameless hotel in Juliaca my not-quite-finished Dorothy Sayers novel, a crossword puzzle book, and my blow dryer.

251

I was bone tired. I lay on the sunken mattress snuggled between Jane and Michael and was filled with an indescribable contentment.

All too soon it was time to go to the train station. I borrowed a scrap of soap from Bob and in the cold water of the basin tried to wash some of the dust of the journey off our face and hands. We gathered our few belongings and crossed the street, dodging bicycle carts, honking cars, and pedestrians. Inside the dimly lit station we crowded into line. To one side, a group of Australian campers stood around a veritable mountain of gear. The rest of our fellow travelers were Peruvians, mostly Indians with bundles on their backs and more at their feet.

We waited another hour before boarding. On the tracks there was a confusion of trains, and it took some running back and forth on Bob's part to locate the car whose number was stamped on our tickets. Once inside, Lloyd settled into a wide bench seat, and Jane, Michael, and I sat across from him. There was a table between the two facing seats. Bob sat in the next row. In vain I tried to find a spot to rest my feet in the space under the table, but it was crammed with luggage. It was going to be a long night.

Jane and Michael were excited. It was to be their first train trip.

"Mommy, when is the train going to leave?" Michael asked.

I glanced at my watch. It was 9 P.M. "It should be leaving any minute."

Minutes passed and nothing happened. Our fellow passengers were already snoozing in their seats, covered up to their noses with blankets and ponchos. A bare bulb dangling from the ceiling pierced the gloom. The children and I watched eagerly out the window at the people hurrying to and fro. Half an hour passed. With a lurch the train finally started.

The kids pressed their noses against the window. "Yay, we're leaving!"

The train slowly rolled backward for a few hundred yards. Then it stopped. There it remained for twenty or thirty minutes while more people boarded. Then it started again and proceeded back to the station, where it stopped again.

"Why does the train keep stopping? When are we going to leave?" Jane and Michael kept asking. Lloyd didn't know. Bob didn't know. I didn't know.

Over the next two hours, the train went back and forth half a dozen times. By then it was so crowded that people were standing in the aisles. Some of them had spread out makeshift beds on the floor, and newly boarding passengers had to pick their way among the sleeping bodies. It was 11:30 P.M. when we finally left the station. The children had long since fallen asleep, and Bob, Lloyd, and I had exhausted our supply of jokes about being in the Twilight Zone, doomed never to leave the Juliaca train station. I was grateful for Bob's alpaca rug, which had been pressed into service as a sleeping bag. Lloyd and I had wrapped Michael in it, and he lay asleep on the table like a giant cocoon. Jane was curled up beside me on the seat with her head in my lap.

For hours I watched through the window as the train passed through a shadowy landscape of moonlit mountains. Sometimes flat pools of water glinted in the moonlight. There were no towns, no houses, no living thing in sight, not even a tree. We were above the timberline. The train stopped every once in a while for more passengers, who seemed to appear out of nowhere. Frosty air seeped through the window glass. My teeth chattered, and my feet were like blocks of ice. For once I was glad I was wearing a wig—it helped keep my head warm. Across from me Lloyd snored softly, his head bowed onto his chest. As the train rolled on into the night, time seemed to stand still. It began to seem as if I had always been on that train and would never get off again.

Chapter Eighteen

Saturday, April 30, 1988

As the first light of morning came through the windows, brakes squealed and the train lurched to a stop. It was 5 A.M. People began to stir. Bob stood up and stretched. "I've got butt-itis," he griped, then repeated it in Spanish, to the amusement of our fellow passengers. Jane sat up and rubbed her eyes.

"Are we there yet?"

"Not yet."

"Where are we?" I didn't know. Nowhere, as far as I could tell.

An hour passed. Then someone tramped by outside our windows, shouting, "Trasborde! Trasborde!"

The Peruvians quickly began gathering their bundles and pushing off the train. There was mass confusion.

"What's going on?" Bob asked someone.

"We're transferring to another train."

"No," someone else said, "We're supposed to stay put. There's another train on the way. We have to wait for it."

"What's wrong with our train?"

No one knew. Finally we joined the crowd bustling off the train. It seemed they were heading for another train that was waiting to take us the rest of the way to Arequipa. The ground outside was white and crunchy with frost. I took the largest duffle bag, Michael shouldered the smaller one, and Jane carried my purse slung across her thin shoulders. The Peruvians were sliding down the steep embankment and scurrying across the flatter terrain below us. Lloyd and Bob followed suit. I knew I couldn't make it down the embankment with Jane and Michael—they'd be too afraid of falling, and I didn't have spare hands to hold onto them with. We'd have to pick our way alongside the tracks.

There was scarcely room to walk single file with the train on one side and the embankment dropping off on the other. Jane and Michael whimpered with fear but said nothing as they slipped and stumbled over the rocky, frozen ground. Our hands were soon black with soot from clutching at the sides of the train to keep from falling. We rounded a curve in the tracks and I saw why the train could not go on: four cars, including the two engines, had derailed and were leaning outward at a precarious angle. I shivered as I looked next to us over a cliff which fell hundreds of feet down the mountainside. If the cars had derailed completely, they might have pulled the whole train over the cliff with them, with us inside.

We caught up with Bob and Lloyd at the replacement train. They were leaning on their luggage and surveying the scene.

"This train is a lot smaller," said Bob. "Eight cars smaller."

The Peruvians had sized up the situation with practiced quickness, and the new train was already full and overflowing. Still more passengers swirled around us looking for cars that had enough space to hold them. People were jammed inside some of the cars so that the doors were impossible to open. There were no railroad employees in sight to try to make order out of the chaos.

"I'll go check again to see if there's one we can get on," Bob said. He returned red-faced and panting.

"There's no room anywhere," he puffed. "We've got to get on one of these." I looked at the Peruvians pushing and shoving onto the cars in front of us. Then I looked around at the bleak icy landscape—a sort of frozen tundra surrounded by craggy mountains—and for a crazy moment considered staying and waiting for the next train. But there wouldn't be another train for at least twelve hours, and there was no food or shelter here. Besides, somewhere in those mountains bands of terrorists lurked. I weighed the prospect of being stranded with the children in this remote spot with the prospect of being crushed inside the train.

There was no time to think. Steam started puffing from between the wheels. Lloyd shouted, "Get on now!" and he and Bob headed for one of the coaches. I hoisted the duffle bags onto my shoulder, grabbed the children's hands, and ran for the nearest coach. People were blocking the doorway and hanging off the steps. I pushed a white-faced Jane and Michael onto the steps ahead of me and clung to the handrail with one hand. Metal screamed on metal and the train jolted into movement. I swung precariously from the bottom step. Then brown hands reached down and pulled Jane and Michael to safety on the landing, and the wall of bodies parted enough for me to follow them. I pushed Jane and Michael ahead of me through the door of the coach, then we picked our way over bundles and bodies to the middle of the car. For a few moments I gripped Jane's and Michael's hands and we stood swaying to the movement of the train, wedged in too tightly to fall. Then a teenager took Michael onto her lap and someone cleared a space on the table for Jane to sit. A bespectacled university student gave me his bundle to sit on in the aisle.

It was 6:30 a.m. We were still five hours away from Arequipa.

Jane and Michael were wide awake now and over their fright. Michael took out his transformer truck and kept up a nonstop stream of chatter in Spanish, entertaining all the passengers within earshot. Latin Americans dote on children, and the Peruvians were delighted with these little gringos who talked and sang in perfect Spanish. Jane contentedly played with her Skipper doll and drew pictures with a box of pencils that we dug out of the duffle bag. My fellow passengers talked quietly or dozed. No one complained. Like Bolivians, they accepted even the most chaotic situations with equanimity. I admired their endurance, but couldn't help daydreaming about the glories of a shower, a bed, and a meal.

Two hours later Jane looked at me with a pale, miserable face and said, "Mommy, I don't feel good." I had forgotten that she had a tendency to get carsick. In fact, it was amazing that it hadn't happened sooner on

258

this trip. Thank heaven for small favors. I took out the one Kleenex I had left and snatched Michael's woolen cap off his head to press it into service as a motion sickness bag. There was nowhere to take her, so Jane threw up where she sat. Instantly people were helpful, clearing more space on the table for her to lie down, opening the window for fresh air, producing a plastic bag to line Michael's dripping cap with. Jane lay on the table for the rest of the trip, eyes closed, clutching the cap, wretching occasionally. All I could do was pat her hand and shield her face from the sun coming through the window. The endless journey continued; the train rolled on.

Finally, at 11 A.M., three hours behind schedule, we arrived at the Arequipa station. We had been on the train for fourteen hours. I scanned the jostling crowd for Lloyd and Bob and then spotted them, rumpled and unshaven, standing by their mound of luggage. They grinned and gave the thumbs up. We looked at each others' road-weary faces and laughed, giddy with relief at finally escaping the train from hell.

Outside the station, Lloyd surveyed with distaste the beat-up taxi that Bob had hailed.

"Don't they have something bigger than that?"

Bob said with exasperation, "This is all there is, Lloyd! There *ain't* nothin' else! We're not in Houston, you know." Lloyd grumbled, but we took the taxi.

Arequipa was tidy and clean-swept, without a beggar or sidewalk vendor in sight, and its streets were lined with whitewashed buildings. Bob explained that in Peru there was a government ban on public begging. The taxi driver asked if we were interested in seeing the Virgin of something-or-other, apparently a local tourist attraction. Bob said irritably, "No, no, the last thing I'm interested in right now is a virgin."

The taxi took us to a fine old hotel on the main square, surrounded by elegant colonial buildings. Bob registered himself, me, and the kids under his name, as if we were a family, and Lloyd registered separately in the room next door.

The first order of business was food. We dumped our luggage in the room and then headed straight for the restaurant. Since leaving Juliaca, the children and I had not eaten or drunk anything except a small can of guayaba juice that we'd shared on the train.

We sat outside on the hotel's upper veranda, which ran the length of the hotel, a full block long, and looked out over the main plaza. Bob ordered a dozen bottles of water and vast quantities of food. Michael and Jane ran up and down the veranda, working off all the pent-up energy and tension of the past eighteen hours. Bob said they reminded him of balloons zipping around with the air let out of them. It seemed incredible that it had been only a day and a half since we'd left La Paz.

Lloyd, who was usually fastidious about his food, told us how on the train he'd devoured part of a grimy orange that had been passed the length of the car to him via who-knows-how-many dirty hands and had already been nibbled on by who-knows-how-many strange mouths. We laughed as he recounted how he'd stood up all the way to Arequipa, propping up the mountain of gear belonging to the Australian camping group. It seemed that the people in their car, too, had developed a kind of temporary camaraderie and help-fulnesss — the kind that occurs in a crisis among people

260

who would otherwise have nothing in common.

After lunch we all went to our rooms and napped. I was disappointed that the room had two single beds instead of a double; I was getting used to sleeping cuddled up with my long-lost babies. But the disappointment passed quickly. Maybe because I hadn't slept in two days, the narrow bed with its scratchy blanket felt delicious. Just being horizontal was a blissful sensation. I started tingling from head to toe as my sluggish blood, which seemed to have congealed in a frozen slush somewhere near my feet, began flowing upward again. I knew that from then on, I would only have to remember how it felt to sit up all night on the train, and I'd be able to lie down and happily sleep anywhere.

We ate supper at a Chinese restaurant that Bob had discovered just around the corner from the hotel. We dallied at a toy store on the way, and Lloyd bought Jane a stuffed kitten and Michael a Winnie the Pooh. In the restaurant, again we ordered piles of food, most of which remained uneaten.

Afterward, Lloyd and I strolled around the plaza with the children. They raced here and there, but I didn't let them get more than 50 feet out of reach. Meanwhile Bob went to check out the flight situation. He found that in Arequipa, as in Juliaca, all flights to Lima were booked for several days.

Back at the hotel we enjoyed more luxuries: hot showers, clean towels, and flush toilets. Through the window Jane and Michael watched the antics of a family of alley cats on the roof next door. We were finally safe, I thought.

Chapter Nineteen

Sunday, May 1, 1988

Early in the morning, as we were getting ready for breakfast, Lloyd knocked at the door. He told the kids to wait in the next room with Bob, then sat down and began, "I don't want to alarm you, but . . ." He told me that the previous night he and Bob had called their wives long distance. "My wife got a phone call from Guy's son. He told her that Guy had called him from Bolivia. Apparently Guy couldn't say much, but he did say he was in a lot of trouble and needed $10,000 in cash to get out."

Oh, no, they'd caught Guy.

"We figure he was arrested in La Paz, maybe at the airport on Saturday morning. They probably traced him to the rented Jeep. As soon as we get out of here, Bob's going back to La Paz to try to get him out." I swallowed, dismayed. Lloyd went on, "And in spite of Bob's carefree attitude, we're not out of the woods yet. Down at the desk some police—probably from Interpol — were going over the hotel register and asking a lot of questions. It was about something that happened in Bolivia on Friday." My throat went dry.

"How did you find out about that?"

"Bob just happened to be standing there at the desk when the police came up." An involuntary shiver ran down my spine.

"We found out something else too. The train derailed because terrorists dynamited the tracks." He paused while this sank in. So the Sendero Luminoso *had* been in those hills. "We've been lucky so far. But our luck could run out at any time. We're not going to wait around here any longer. As soon as we get some breakfast, we're going to leave for the airport and we're going to get on a plane *today*. We've got to get out of here." He stood up and glowered at me. "Whatever happens, don't let go of those children. If we have to, Bob and I will get physical." Then he left.

The room swam for a moment. All the tension and terror of the past two days came flooding back. Mustn't show it. Must be calm and cheerful for the children. I could hear their chirping voices through the thin wall from the room next door. I remained seated on the bed until the wild beating of my heart slowed down. Then I stood up to gather the children and go down to breakfast.

In the hotel coffee shop we played the role of tourists. Bob asked a man at the next table to take a picture of us: Lloyd smiling proudly, I in my now rather disheveled wig, Jane and Michael grinning above plates of pancakes, and Bob wearing a t-shirt with "Miami" in six-inch letters spread across his ample belly.

Waving his fork enthusiastically, Bob began to discuss the possibility of rescuing Guy from the La Paz prison with a hot air balloon.

"The good thing about hot air balloons is that no matter how many holes get shot into them, they'll still fly," he chuckled. He was all but rubbing his hands together at the prospect.

"You really thrive on this stuff, don't you?" I asked.

"Yeah, I guess I do. Maybe I watched too much *Mission: Impossible* when I was a kid."

"No, you're just nuts, that's all. Both of you," I laughed. Maybe the fact that they could make jokes about Guy's predicament was part of what made them good at what they did. After all, crying and wringing their hands wouldn't do him any good. Soon I was joking along with them. Maybe I was going a little bit nuts myself.

In minutes we arrived at the entrance to the airport. The gatekeeper waved us to one side, and a grim-faced policeman advanced. He peered through the window studying our faces. I waited, scarcely breathing. *Now* what? The policeman ordered the driver to open the trunk and Bob jumped out of the taxi too. Lloyd said nothing. His face betrayed no emotion.

As they searched the trunk, I prayed the now-familiar prayer, "Dear God, not now. We're so close — don't let me lose them now." Bob and the driver got back in the taxi and we pulled away.

"He was looking for arms," Bob explained. "Apparently a lot of guns are being smuggled in for the Sendero Luminoso." I let out my breath and tightened my grip on the children's hands. How many more such moments were left before we were really home free?

The airport was small but busy, with people crowding around the ticket counters. I waited with Lloyd at one of the counters while Bob went briskly back and forth among the various airlines trying to get tickets to Lima. Apparently a lot of other people had the same idea.

I sat the kids on the floor, out of sight behind the luggage, and positioned myself next to them. If someone was looking for a tall gringa, I was not going to make it easy for them.

Bob managed to get us on the waiting list on every flight leaving for Lima that morning. Finally, a bribe of $60 convinced the AeroPeru agent to simply scratch five paid passengers off his list and pencil in our names instead. The flight would be leaving in twenty-five minutes.

As we waited in line to board, Jane slipped away. I looked around for her in panic. Bob nudged me gently and pointed. There she was—a small hooded figure in baggy jeans two sizes too big, kneeling with folded hands before a Catholic shrine in the corner. She quietly rejoined us a moment later. Afterward, I asked what she had been praying for, and she said, "For a safe trip home."

We were first in line to board. I sat in the aisle seat and immediately buckled Jane and Michael into the seats beside me. "Keep their seatbelts buckled at all times, so nobody can grab them out of their seats," Lloyd said. It was 9:40 A.M.

The stewardess passed around the Lima newspapers and I scanned the international headlines for news of the kidnapping. Nothing. It was Sunday, May 1—Labor Day in Bolivia—and the country was still plagued with nationwide strikes and turmoil on the eve of the

Pope's visit. Lloyd commented that we'd escaped Bolivia in the nick of time. With the escalating unrest, the borders would clamp down until after the Pope left.

Bob and Lloyd studied flight schedules. The next flight to Miami wouldn't be until Monday. We'd have to spend the night in Lima. They were uneasy about it — Lima was the logical place for someone to watch for us, since it was the only city in Peru with flights to the United States. During the flight Michael peppered me with questions about an in-flight comic book he was looking at.

It was 11 A.M. when we landed in Lima.

"Bob," Lloyd said, "you get off the plane ahead of us and do some reconnoitering. See if somebody's hanging around watching for us. If there is, distract him."

Lloyd, the children, and I stayed in our seats while everyone else disembarked. Then, holding tightly to Jane's and Michael's hands, I followed Lloyd off the plane and into the terminal. He was walking briskly, and we half ran to keep up with him. I glanced around the concourse. Bob was nowhere in sight.

Then, about a hundred yards ahead of us, Bob appeared, waving us on. Lloyd broke into a trot, and we followed suit.

"There's an Eastern flight leaving for Miami in twenty minutes!" Bob exclaimed.

At the Eastern counter we turned over our passports and in moments we were booked on the flight. We trotted to the immigration station. This was where we would leave Bob behind — he would be returning to Bolivia to rescue Guy. There was no time for a proper good-bye. I threw my arms around him and we hugged quicky, then he hugged each of the children.

266

" 'Bye, kids. Be good."

Lloyd was motioning impatiently. Shepherding the children in front of me, we hurried to join him in line. I looked back. Bob stood watching us, still wearing his Miami t-shirt and the alpaca hat. He waved, his blue eyes merry. I waved back, blinking back tears. I owed him so much—not only for his part in recovering my children, but for his unflagging good spirits, his kindness, his encouragement. When I looked back again, he was gone.

The children and I were passed along from desk to desk and picked up our passports at the last one. We hurried around the corner to the boarding gate to wait for Lloyd. He had been delayed for some reason.

Seconds passed. The boarding gate was empty; all the other passengers had already boarded. I kept an anxious eye on Jane and Michael as they skipped up and down. Something's wrong, I thought. Why was Lloyd taking so long? Unable to stand the suspense any longer, I started back to see what the holdup was. Around the corner he appeared, trench coat flapping.

Outside the plane's engines began to whine, and then the whine rose to a roar. Customs inspectors quickly zipped open our luggage and felt around inside. They zipped them back up and handed them to us. I slung the duffle bags around my neck, grabbed Jane's and Michael's hands, and hurried onto the tarmac behind Lloyd. The plane was a hundred feet in front of me. I fixed my eyes on it and started to run, expecting any moment to feel a detaining hand on my arm. Then we were up the steps and inside the plane. I took the aisle seat across from Lloyd and put the kids by the window. The plane started to taxi away from the airport, then turned back toward the terminal.

Lloyd whispered ominously, "The plane's turning back."

I ignored him. It couldn't be—the plane was simply turning down another runway. And indeed it was. As it picked up speed and took off, Lloyd and I slapped hands across the aisle in a high-five.

Eastern Airlines was celebrating some kind of anniversary and they passed out complimentary bottles of wine to all the passengers. I looked next to me at Jane and Michael. They were already asleep in their seats, their uptilted faces full of peace and trust. I lifted the wine in a silent toast and drank it to the dregs.

Epilogue

It would make for a nice neat ending to say that we lived happily ever after. But life is never that simple. After spending the night in Miami, Lloyd, the children, and I flew on to Texas. I hadn't dared to go to my parents, so instead the children and I stayed with friends for a few weeks. Only a handful of people knew where we were: my family, a few friends, and, of course, Mr. Rosenthal.

I was euphoric for the first few weeks after our grand adventure. The children bubbled over with excitement. "That was fun, Mommy! When can we do it again?" they'd say, and I'd smile indulgently and shudder inwardly. I believe that Jane and Michael were in a state of elation for awhile, too. I showered them with attention and affection such as I hadn't done since they were babies. As a matter of principle I'd never allowed them to sleep in my bed at night. But we were forced due to circumstances during the trip and for awhile afterwards to sleep together. I found it wonderfully comforting to wake up at night and feel them cradled one on each side of me and listen to the soft rhythm of their breathing. It

269

was a very close time for us, a time of rebuilding the bond that had been strained, but never broken. I had thought my children were lost to me forever, and they'd been miraculously given back to me. Truly a gift.

It wasn't long, though, before I had to get my head out of the clouds and make some serious decisions about our future. Where would we live now? What did I need to do to cover my tracks? How would I support myself and the children?

I pondered what to do next. Lloyd had advised me to disappear in Los Angeles or New York City, but, after all this time away, I couldn't bring myself to leave my family and friends in Texas. So I compromised. We did move to a large city, but it wasn't New York or L.A. With Mr. Rosenthal's connections, I had several interviews and found a good job right away. Jane, Michael, and I settled into our new life and began again — new city, new home, new school, new job, new friends for them and for me, a new start. Even a new identity. Following at least part of Lloyd's advice, I changed my name and took other measures to make it as difficult as possible for Federico to find us again.

Starting over was exciting, and for the first time in years I knew that things were finally falling into place for me — for us. At the same time it was terribly frightening. I had never been on my own before — there had always been parents, or roommates, or a husband — and now I had not only myself but also two children that I was completely responsible for. The burden of being the only breadwinner and somehow making ends meet, of trying to be both mother and father to my children, of making the thousands of decisions, large and small, that went into running a household —

schools, daycare, church, doctors, schedules, meals, clothes—and somehow here and there squeezing in a few precious moments for myself—was (and still is) sometimes overwhelming, as I'm sure all single working mothers (and fathers, for that matter) know.

And I felt so alone at first. I knew not a soul in this big new city and dared not confide in anyone. To fill the solitary hours after the children were in bed, I began writing this book. I wanted to have a family chronicle of our "grand adventure" while the scenes and conversations were still fresh in my memory. The handful of people who knew the story encouraged me to write it down. They were amazed at the uncanny chain of events that had brought me and the children safely out of South America and home again. Even Lloyd was surprised. On the flight to Miami from Lima he'd told me that our chances were "less than zero," and that in all his years with the FBI and as a private investigator, he'd never seen anything like it.

We had been incredibly lucky. But we hadn't escaped totally unscathed. In a routine preschool check, Michael tested positive for tuberculosis, which is still widespread in Bolivia. For a year he took daily medication and was closely followed by a doctor. And Jane had to start all over again in the first grade, having missed all but two months of it the previous year.

But our most abiding legacy was fear—fear that Federico could find us and take the children again. If I stepped out of their line of vision in the supermarket, Jane or Michael would yell "Mommy!" in a panicky voice. When they played outside, I would stand nearby, watching with suspicion anyone who came too near. I coached the children carefully about strangers and, of course, about their father, should he unexpectedly show up. I could see in their eyes that it was a difficult lesson. Michael said, "If I see Daddy, I might forget and run up and hug him." He added quickly, "But after I hug him, I'll run away." It was wrenching. I didn't want them to grow up fearing their father. Yet they had to be aware that it could happen again.

Federico hadn't taken their departure lightly. Within days of their disappearance, he'd filed lawsuits against everyone that might have had anything to do with it: me, of course, Dr. Castillo, Russ and Food Aid International. He'd even lodged a complaint against the U.S. Consulate, accusing them of being accomplices to my plans. I found all this out in June 1988, when I received a letter from Dr. Castillo, forwarded by Mr. Rosenthal. Dr. Castillo sent copies of two issues of *Criterio,* a news magazine published in Bolivia. Featured on the cover of the May 23, 1988, issue was a photograph of Jane and Michael, and an article entitled, "The Kidnapping of the Bascope Children." Inside, a six-page story described how doting father Freddy Bascope had "rescued" his children from their neglectful American mother and returned them to the bosom of their homeland, Bolivia, where they were living happily until they were violently snatched away by me.

The article was full of half-truths, lies, and conveniently forgotten details, including the fact that Federico had illegally kidnapped the children in the first place. In the article the *Criterio* reporter described his interview with the U.S. Consul. Since Steven Dunlop was out of town, another official was interviewed. He explained that all the Consulate did was to issue passports for the Bascope children, which was their right as U.S.

citizens. He, of course, denied any involvement with the kidnapping. When asked by the reporter about the mother's "immoral behavior" as described in Mr. Bascope's lawsuit, he responded rather stiffly that in the United States, citizens had a right to privacy and that the U.S. government didn't keep files on them.

Even the nun from Amor de Dios school was interviewed. She claimed that I escaped with the children by shoving her out of the way. In view of all the uproar, I could understand why even a woman of the cloth would try to protect herself. At least she had done the right thing when it mattered. It seemed apt that her name was "Esperanza," which means "hope" in Spanish.

The article included photographs of the gate we'd passed through, the bathroom I'd hidden in, and the apartment where I'd stayed. They'd recovered a photo I.D. of Bob and his registration at the Hotel Claudia, showing that he'd checked in on April 4, 1988, and checked out at 8 A.M. on April 29. There was even a photo of the crude map I'd drawn of the school grounds, which I'd left behind in my suitcase, where the Bolivian police discovered it.

As soon as the first article appeared, Dr. Castillo had marched to the *Criterio* offices and attempted to clear his name. He explained that he couldn't have had anything to do with the resnatch because he was in Sucre presenting my case to the Supreme Court that day. He showed the *Criterio* reporter my legal documents and pointed out that Federico had illegally kidnapped the children himself, and that he was wanted in the U.S. by the FBI. This put a whole different light, albeit not as interesting and sensational a one, on the affair, and gave rise to a second article appearing in the May 30 issue. This was a cover feature, too, called, "Kidnap of the Bascope Children: The Other Version." In the article it was admitted that Dr. Castillo's revelations cast Federico's version of events "in serious question."

In his letter to me, Dr. Castillo said that I had put him in a difficult position (not mentioning that I had done exactly what he'd advised me to do), and that under the circumstances I should immediately send him $5,000 in U.S. currency to help him with his legal expenses. I wrote him back, telling him that I regretted the pickle he was in, that of course he had had nothing to do with my actions, but that I wasn't going to send him any money. At least, I thought, he could use my letter as evidence of his innocence. I never heard from him again.

Although I never learned how Dr. Castillo extricated himself from his legal difficulties, I do know about most of the other people involved in my story.

After he was arrested in the Plaza Hotel in La Paz, Guy was held under house arrest and interrogated for 48 hours. Then, with the help of $10,000 in bribes sent by Lloyd, he was released and returned home to Miami. Food Aid International and Russ were eventually found innocent of any wrongdoing.

Lloyd is still running his private investigation agency in Houston. I was greatly saddened to learn from Lloyd that Bob died in the summer of 1990 from a sudden illness.

My friend Susan is still living and working in McAllen. Kathy has moved to New Mexico. She and her husband have added another boy to the family. Mr. Rosenthal continues practicing law in McAllen, and we keep in touch.

Courtney, my father and stepmother, my brothers, and the rest of my family are doing well and are as close as ever.

As for Federico, he is still on the FBI list and cannot get a visa to return to the United States. A few months after I recovered the children, he wrote a letter to my parents. In it he said that I must have loved Jane and Michael very much to have done what I did to get them back and that he wouldn't do anything to upset their lives any further. On their birthdays and at Christmas he sends cards to them through a relative's address. Federico seems to be content living in Bolivia and pursuing his career in the textile business.

I wish him well. After all, the happier he is, the less I have to worry about. You might think that as the victor I can afford to be magnanimous, that as the winner I have the luxury of pitying the loser. But it is the children who have lost the most. They still love their father, and they still miss him. Michael summed it up when he said, "Mommy, when I was with Daddy I missed you, and now that I'm with you, I miss Daddy."

There is no winner. No real solution.